# JAY JAX

## 1936

By: R. A. FEDAK

INK START MEDIA
5710 W Gate City Blvd Ste K #284
Greensboro, NC 27407

# Chapter One

June 1, 1936

The door to Jay's office creaked as Alice cautiously opened it. It was early morning and a bright sunny day and seventy degrees in San Franci-sco. But the room was dark. As Alice crept toward the window, she kicked a bottle of bourbon across the linoleum floor. Looks like Jay had another one of his nights. The young woman stood at the window for a moment, a wry grin growing on her petty face. She pulled the paper shade slowly down an inch, then she let go of it, and it flew to the top of the roller, slapping around making a racket. The bright sun lit up the room.

Jay jumped up from his desk, where he had been sleeping on his arms.

He was a mess, hair standing up, dark circles under his eyes. "What the..."

Alice was laughing.

"Very funny, Jay moaned as he dropped his head back into his arms. "Morning bright eyes, your mail is on the desk. Here's your coffee," she said as she placed a cup of coffee before him.

He took a sip, then groggily he searched for his WWI bayonet which he used as a letter opener. He opened his first three letters, which turned out to be bills. The fourth caught his eye, he reached for it carefully. It was from his Italian buddy, who fought in the last war.

May 17, 1936

Dear Jay

Been a long-time my friend. As you know, the Opera Company is finishing its last leg of are world tour. On June 6th we will be in San Francisco. Here are two tickets June 6th performance at the Opera House. I need to see you after the performance. Give me 15 to 20 minutes before you come up to my dressing room. Make sure that you bring Alice. I always enjoy her company.

Captain Giovanni Mattola

Jay could tell that something was wrong. His old friend never signs his letter with his military rank. He always signed Gio. Jay looked closer at the envelope. It was post marked Honolulu, Hawaii. Jay knew that his old friend was on a world tour that started in Italy and was ending in Berlin.

He called to Alice in the outer office, "doing anything next Saturday?"

"What do have in mind?"

"Giovanni sent us tickets to the opera. He wants to see us. Call Goldman's Tailor Shop and tell Jacob that I need a tux for that night." Jay then tact the tickets to his calendar.

When Jay finished his coffee, Jay pulled his Emson Camera out of his middle desk drawer. The camera was a small one, fitting easily in the palm of his hand. "It's still nine days till next Saturday. Meantime, I got to make a living," he mumbled to himself."

Four days ago, a beautiful blonde, stacked, mid-twenties had sauntered into his office. Everything about her was expensive, even her perfume. According to her story, she thought that her husband was cheating on her. She hired Jay to follow her husband. When Jay heard the name and figured out that her husband was sixty-six-year-old oil and railroad tycoon A.J. Wainsford, he said, "what makes you think that he's cheating?"

She crossed her long, sleek legs in a whisper of silk and said, "well he comes home late, or doesn't come home at all."

"Rich guys have lots of habits. That doesn't mean he's cheating."

She was wearing a really thin full-length sweater, and when she reached ink for her belt, his heart skipped a beat. She flung it open. She had a tight blouse under it. "Look at this body. Would you find some hussy?" Catching his breath, he said, "I see your point. Okay, I'll shadow him for a few days, and we'll see what comes up. There's probably a good explanation. Getting up from the visitor's chair, she said, "I hope you're right." After she left, Alice peeked in, a big grin on her face. Before s any words came out of, he mouth. He said, "Shad up." He himself had a little grin on his face.

It was a nice day, so Jay walked the eight blocks to Wainsford office building on the corner of Sansome and Clay Streets and took up a position on a sidewalk bench across the street. He had his usual prop, the morning paper. Lunch was a Coke and a hotdog smothered in kraut from a passing vender. He was told that Wainsford always went to lunch promptly at noon. It was now 11:30. A minute past noon he emerged from his building, walked up to the corner and made a left. Jay folded his paper and fell in step behind him, keeping to the store-fronts side of the street so he could feign window shopping if he had to.

On the next block, the old man went into Sal's Restaurant. Jay crossed the street and shifted in his tourist mode, where he began taking pictures. While no woman appeared, a man did. He was short and a little heavy. Jay saw him join Wainsford table, there were two other men with him. Jay decided to enter the restaurant, where he sat at the mahogany bar with the multi-colored bottles behind it. He began nursing a bourbon. Neat, he was sitting about ten feet from Wainsford's table and his guests. They were talking, mostly about money. Jay had learned a long time ago, the art of concentrating on a conversation. He was able to block extraneous noise and focus on the conversation.

Soon he was getting an earful, hard to believe. Did people really talked that way? The heavy-set man said, "my last royalty was only seventy-five thousand. It was an off week. I don't think that I'm charging clients enough."

The meeting ended a little after one o'clock. Jay sat there till Nine-thirty the evening. While he sat there, Jay was wondering how Alice was doing with her case. She was working on an actual cheating husband. Mrs. Edna Longmire hired her to catch her cheating husband in the act. Alice was making pretty good head way with her case. She actually had a few drinks with her husband. Alice said that the man takes off his wedding ring every time they met. Being it was summertime, his skin was dark with a suntan, except on his left ring finger. He might as well have a sign hanging from his neck saying, I CHEAT ON MY WIFE.

Meanwhile, Jay was ready to call it a night. Most of the Wainsford Building was dark, except for his twelfth-floor office lights. Jay decided to go into the building across the street from Wainsford's building, which was fifteen stories. He took the back stairs up to the roof. The only problem was avoiding any janitor or maintenance personnel as he went to the roof. After making it to the roof without incident. It was cold and getting windy as he leveled his binoculars on Wainsford's office. He was there at his plush desk, eating.

Forty-five minutes later the man got up from his desk and went into another room of his office suite, where he glanced out the window. After a while he lays down on an office lounge chair, and since he taken off his shoes, it looked like he was retiring for the night.

Jay decided to go home, meaning his office. Tomorrow, he told himself he would bring his car. The after he finishes his surveillance, he would be able to go home, instead of his office.

The next day the tycoon's routine didn't vary from the day before. Lunch at Sal's meeting with business associates, and this time he left his office at about six o' clock. Jay fell in behind his big Bentley and followed. Strange, Jay thought, a multi-millionaire dives himself.

He went straight home. This left Jay scratching his head. "Odd. Very odd. I'd like to hear him explain his last two nights to his wife," He chuckled as he set out for home.

# Chapter Two

The weekend was uneventful. Jay stopped at O'Malley's to have a few drinks with his friend Lt. Mike Morris, he was a San Francisco cop, burglary and homicide. Jay was in the war with Mike and worked as a Sargent with the police force.

When Jay told him about his current case involving Ann Wainsford Mike reacted with unabashed vehemence. "Baloney, "he said. I've known A.J. for over ten years. We met when I was investigating a break in, resulting of the murder of his butler. His first wife died of cancer five years ago. A.J. was angry and lost without his Mary. He met Ann when he was in New York for an oil conference. He met with Rockefeller, Carnegie, Vanderbilt, and others.

After the conference, the went to a Broadway show, Ann was a dancer in the show. He went backstage with two dozen roses; He was like a schoolboy. He asked Ann if she would like to go to dinner. Of course, she said okay. Two years later they were married. It was the biggest social event of the year. Me and my wife were in the bridal party. We weren't really sure how to act in front of all these rich people." Jay said, "okay I heard of that wedding. Wasn't that when I was still in the hospital?"

"It was. He would never cheat on her, why should he? You have seen her," Mike asked. Jay replied, "yes, I have seen her. I know what you mean." Mike added, "if he is coming home late, oh staying out all night, I'm sure there's a good explanation."

That personal input from a friend put this matter in a different light for Jay. Now he was more intrigued than ever with this case. Mike asked if Jay would keep him in the loop. "By the way, a couple of days ago I got a letter from Giovanni. His opera is performing at the Opera House on the 6th. Mike asked, "how is the old baritone?"

Jay cocked his head. "I'm not sure. He said that he wanted to see me after the performance Saturday night. There was something odd about the letter. Ya know what I mean. It just didn't sound like him, his letters are always upbeat, this one is dark. He also signed it Captain Giovanni Mattola. He never signed with his rank before. Some things up. Well, Saturday night I'll be in my office working on the First National Bank robbery and when the guard was shot last weekend. I can't figure out how three men get in, kill a guard and get out without a trace. Tell the maestro that we'll meet in my office after the performance. It will be great to see him again. Last time I saw him was at your wedding." Mike bit his lip when he realized what he said. Jay can see that he was upset. "Don't worry about that Mike, I'm okay," Jay assured him. Jay decided to leave. He left and left Mike to pay the bill. Their always doing things like that from one and another.

On Monday Morning, Jay picked up the routine on the Wainsford case.

And again, Wainsford followed the same routine as last week. Jay muttered to himself, "if he has a woman stashed somewhere, he's doing a great job of hiding her. It's been three days."

It was time to confront the man. When A.J. left the restaurant, Jay followed him for about a block, and then closed in on him, he moved along side of him and said, Mr. Wainsford."

The man turned to him and locked eyes. Jay took measure of the man.

He didn't balk, or hesitate, or avoided eyes, but simply said, "yes can I help you?" Jay said, "you don't know me, but I'm a Private Investigator, my name is Jay Jax.

Wainsford seemed a little surprised. "What would a P.I. want with me?"

Jay said, "let me be blunt. I was hired by your wife."

Now incredulous, Wainsford said, "Alice hired you." He paused. "For what?"

"Well," Jay started, "it seems that she is concerned about you coming home late, or not at all. She convinced that there's another woman. I've been following you for three days, and if there in another woman. I'd like to know how you're hiding her. I haven't seen anything. Can you tell me what the hell's going on? Why the sleeping in your office Thursday night?

"It's nothing like that. Obviously, you've seen Ann. Beautiful, isn't she?" Jay nodded. "That's why I was wondering why someone your age, married to a twenty-year-old would cheat on a woman who looks like Ann."

Wainsford started walking, Jay right alongside. "There's no girlfriend. When my Mary died, I thought that I would die myself. I'm not cheating. I love her dearly. When I was in New York at a conference, Rockefeller wouldn't take no for an answer when the decided to take in a Broadway show. Ann was in the show, I know it's corny, but I think I fell in love with her the second I saw her. After the show I went backstage, with two dozen roses. She wasn't the star of the show, but she was a star to me. The rest is history."

"So," Jay asked, "what's the problem?"

"Maybe you can't see it, maybe you can't see it, but there's a forty-year gap between our ages."

"While I love having sex with her, I'm sixty-five and I don't have the stamina to keep up with her. She wants it just about every night. I'm good, on a good week three times, but that's it. That's why I've been sleeping in my office."

Jay frowned. "Did you ever try explaining this with her. If she loves you, that shouldn't be a problem. I think that you go home tonight and let her know."

"I know your right; I'll tell her tonight."

Jay said, "I think that's a good idea."

They shook hands cordially and Parted.

Back at the office, Jay Stopped at the photography shop. Rick had all of his photos ready as he walked in. "Alice, can you get Mrs. Wainsford on the phone, please. "Wainsford line two," bellowed Alice.

Jay picked up the phone. "Mrs. Wainsford, I have some information for you. Can you come in at four o'clock?"

"I'll be there?"

At four, she walked into the office. "Mister Jax, Mrs. Wainsford is here," said Alice over the intercom. "Send her in." When she walked into Jay's office, her eyes were red, her makeup slightly streaked. Jay said, "please sit down. Can we get you a cup of coffee or something?"

She sniffed and nodded. Jay spread three days of photographs on his desk. She leaned forward and intently studied the photos. Looking up with query in her eyes, she said, "I don't see any woman."

"And you won't. He loves only one woman, and I believe it's you."

"Then why the hell isn't he coming home at night."

Jay gazed at her. She noticed and lowered her eyes. "This is a delicate matter, Ann. I'm searching for words.

Her eyes dilated. "What? What is it?"

Jay felt like a schoolboy, said, "Well I'd really like to tell you, but I think I'll let A.J. tell you tonight. The only thing that you should think of, is that he really loves you."

"Okay, it's strange but I'll do what you said to do. What do I owe you?"

"Twenty-five a day plus expanses, one roll of film, pus developing. That's eighty dollars.

She handed him the money, and as she was on her way to the door. Jay said, "Remember, he really does love you."

After she left Alice walked into his office. "Jay, how would you like going on a double date tonight?" She asked. Jay asked back, "where and with who?"

"You, me, Mr. And Mrs. Longmire," she told him. "Oh, the case you're working on. Sure, why not, this should be interesting. Where and when," he asked. "Tonight, drinks at the Alibi, later we'll all meet at the Dixie Hotel on Lake Street. I'm going to meet Felix at the Round Oyster Tavern at 7:30. After one or two drinks I'll tell Felix to meet me at the hotel, I'll also tell him that he is going to have the time ever and to be ready, if you know what I mean."

"You know Alice, that you are one scary bitch."

"Well, I learned from the best. Jay at 6:45 you pick up the misses, then I'll meet you in the hotel lobby," she told him. "Okay, boss," Jay said with a chuckle. "I'll bring my camera. Pictures speak the loudest."

Alice told him the plan. She told him to, "have Mrs. Longmire at the hotel at 7:00. Then we'll all make a social call on Mr. Cheater.

Jay asked, "who is this Longmire?" Don't you ever read the paper," she asked. "Haven't you ever heard of The Longmire Publishing Company. He's worth millions."

Oh, okay me and my date will meet you at the hotel at 7:00," Jay told her.

At 6:30 Alice meets Mr. Longmire at the bar. He was sitting at the bar with two drinks in front of him, Alice sits next to him, innocently rubbing his leg with her right hand. She has never seen anyone that was so nervous, and sweaty.

"Alice, I'm glad you made it," Longmire said. "I wouldn't miss this night for a million dollars. You will never forget this night as long as you live." Alice said with the sexiest voice she could conjure up. It was 6:45. Alice says to him, "Why don't you meet me at the hotel. I'll let you get ready, and I'll show up between 7:00 and 7:15."

"Okay, babe, I'll be waiting." He never told Alice his real name, as far as she was concerned His name was Harry Smith. He finished his drink, gave Alice a gentle kiss on her cheek, and left. Alice gave him about ten minutes, then she got up and left to go to the hotel, which was only a block away. About five minutes after she walked into the lobby. Jay came in with Mrs., Longmire.

Alice spoke first, "well, he's up in the room. On the third floor. The one elevator is out of order. So, we have to take the stairs."

Mrs. Longmire says, "that's fine with me. I just want to see that stupid look that he always has on his little fat body.

Jay said, "you must really HATE him."

"Sonny, you have no idea," she said back. At 7:05 they started up the stairs. Jay wasn't saying anything. He was just there to take pictures. They arrived on the floor around 7:08. They made a right from the staircase. They walked down the hallway until they found room 301. Alice made sure that Jay and his date couldn't be seen. Alice softly knocked on the door. You hear from the other side of the door a soft voice, "who is it?" Alice answered, "it's your fantasy and your desirable blond." You could hear him opening the door nervously and slowly. Alice was standing on the left of the door. Harry came into the hall facing Alice never noticing his audience.

He came out into the hallway wearing only his underwear. He might has well been naked. There wasn't much that wasn't showing. "Harry, I have a big surprise for you," she said with a sexy voice. "Great give it to me."

"Okay, close your eyes no peaking. Now turn around. He slowly turned around; Alice never let go of his waist. Alice got closer to him. Ever one could see that he had an erection. "Okay, open your eyes." Just as he opened his eyes, Jay started taking snap shots of the little fat man. Then he sees his soon to be his ex-wife. "Honey let me explain." The Mrs. walked up to him, gently caressing his face. "Don't worry honey," she said with a little passion in her voice. Then she took a couple of steps backward. Her hands were still on his face, he looked up and smiled at the misses. She didn't say a word, then she kicked him in the nuts. He fell to the floor moaning and groaning. Then she said, "You'll hear from my lawyer. Then she started walking towards the stairs. As she walked past Harry a.k.a Felix, she gave him a good kick to his head. Jay and Alice started to leave; Jay had to step over Felix who was sprawled on the floor.

They went back to the office. When Mrs. Longmire handed Alice an envelope. She opened it and said, "Mrs. Longmire this is entirely too much."

"Nonsense you earned every penny of it!" Then she left.

Jay asked her, "how much did she give you?"

Alice said with excitement in her voice, "she gave me $1,000.00."

Jay said, "not bad for five days of work."

"Well, I did have to get a little closer to him than I wanted to. The man was disgusting. You figure a man with that much money would have some class. Not him, he was vulgar, a drunk and a few other bad habits.

On Thursday morning, the tailor Jacob Goldman, walked in carrying a tux. Jay tried it on. Goldman said, "not bad. I just have to make a few alterations. Take in a little on the stomach. Looks like you lost some weight. I'll have it back to you tomorrow."

The next day he was back. Jay tried on the tux. Goldman said, "perfect fit. Alice came in at 2:30 holding a gown that she only worn once.

Jay leered. "Just the way I like 'em. Low in the front and bare in the back." He paused before saying, "Alice, you're going to steal the show."

Alice, loving it, pooh-poohed.

Jay hung he tux in his office closet. Jay wasn't used to being in his office alone, Alice was always there. After filing Alice's case, he decided to visit A.J. Wainsford. When he got to The Wainsford Building, he found his way to the elevator, pushed the 12th floor button. The elevator door opened, there was a desk ten feet from the elevator. Behind the desk was his secretary an attractive woman, her name plate said Victoria. Jay walked up to the desk. "Can I help you?" She asked "Yes, I'd like to see Mr. Wainsford."

"Who shale I say is calling?" Tell him it's Mr. Jax."

"Sir, there's a Mr. Jax here to see you."

"Victoria, send him right in."

"You can go in, turn right, down the hall, you can't miss his office."

"Thank you, Victoria,". Jay walked down the hall until he found himself staring at the two largest oak doors that he has ever see. He didn't knock, he just walked right into the office. "Jay, it's good to see you again."

"Mr. Wainsford"

"Knock that Mr. off, we're friends, call me A.J. What can I do for you?"

"Well, nothing really. I just came by to see how you and the misses are doing."

"If it wasn't for you, you saved my marriage."

"So, I guess everything is okay."

"Are you kidding, my marriage is great. You were right, just tell her the truth. I followed your advice. We're having sex two, maybe three times a week. She's showing my things that I never know two people can do."

"That's great, just do me a favor, keep the sex stuff between you and the misses. I'm glad that everything is fine now. Have you heard that the opera is putting on a show on Saturday and Sunday?

The baritone star of the opera is an old friend of mine, Giovanni Mattola."

"Yes, I heard. You know that I saw the Maestro Mattola a couple of years ago when I was doing business in London."

"Mr.....I mean A.J. I was wondering if you and Ann want to join us?"

"I would love to Jay, except I made plans to take Ann way for the weekend."

"Okay, that's fine. Maybe You could join me for lunch on Monday? At O'Malley's."

"I think that's a good idea. I'll see you Monday."

"Okay, Mr.....A.J."

"You're going to have to work on that."

"I will, see you Monday at noon, 'til then, Bye."

Jay went to his office to get his tux. Jay got his tux and headed home. He took a walk a block from his apartment to get a haircut. Jay walked into Smitty's Barber Show. "Jay, haven't seen you for a while, where you been?"

"You know Smitty, catching cheating husband, cheating wives. You know how it is. Make this cut special, yours truly is going to the opera tomorrow night."

"The opera, well lody da. Moving up in the world Jay."

"Shut your mouth and just cut my hair." Jay said with a chuckle. "You should have been here yesterday. Mike was here. Have you heard from him lately?"

"Yea, I saw him last week." Smitty asked, "did you hear about last night?"

"No, what happened?"

"You know the First National Bank robbery a few weeks ago."

"Yea Mike said that he couldn't figure out how three got into the bank, killed a guard, and got away without leaving a clue. "Well, he found out what happened. It was an inside job. Agnes the head teller, "said Smitty "I have to listen to the news more often."

"It seemed the head teller's boyfriend was the trigger man. She gave him up and the other two. The boyfriend was shot and killed, as soon as that happened the two other guys just gave up." Smitty told him.

Smitty finished Jay's haircut, he paid his forty-five-cents. Then he said, "goodbye." When he got back to his apartment, he gave Alice a call.

Alice answered the phone, "hello."

"Alice it's me. Are you ready for tomorrow?"

"I already showed you my gown of course I'm ready. Had it cleaned and got my hair done."

"Great I just got home from getting my haircut. Okay, the opera starts at 1900. "7:oopm." I'll pick you up around five."

"Why so early if it doesn't start until seven?" She asked. "I just wanted to be there early; I can feel that Gio is in some kind of trouble. I want to be there just to have a look around, see if I see anything out of the ordinary."

"Jay, you have such a suspicious mind." Alice told him. "I just like to be thorough. You never know."

"I guess not."

# Chapter Three

Saturday morning Jay was thinking about giving Giovanni a call at his hotel but thought better of it. One thing Jay knew about Giovanni, He has breakfast and lunch in his room and never talks to anyone Until opening curtain.

At lunch time he met Lt. Mike Morris for lunch and a few drinks at O'Malley's. Mike was already in the bar, sitting in a corner booth. Jay sat across from him. "So, Jay what's up?" Mike asked. "Well in four and a half hours I'm picking up Alice and heading to the Opera House. I have this feeling that Giovanni is in real trouble."

"What makes you think that?"

"It was his letter. The whole letter was wrong. I got many of letters from him over the last eighteen years. I know how he writes that letter just wasn't him."

"Well, Jay I'll be in my office late. Have to do a lot of paperwork on this shooting the other day."

"I heard about that." I have to find how a sweet young teller got mixed up with this looser Wallace "Wally" Williamson. He was a three time looser. I believe that he hooked up with Veronica just so he can case the bank. She told us that they've been together almost six months. She was a sweet kid, now her future is shot."

Jay said, "I guess congratulations are in order."

"So tomorrow when you see Gio tell him that we'll meet for lunch."

"I'll try, but you know his routine."

"That's right, I forgot. Then tell him that I'll see him when he leaves the hotel. Do you know what time they head for the train?"

"I met Mr. Wainsford today. Being he owns the railroad I'll ask him."

"Okay, I'll see you guys Monday morning." Mike told him. "Okay, see you Monday, Mike." Jay went back to his apartment to get ready for tonight's Opera. At four fifteen he left to pick up Alice. On the way to Alice's, he was surprised that the Sunday night traffic was so light.

He got to Alice's around 4:40. Went into her apartment building and rang her bell. The apartment building just installed a new intercom system. "Who is it," she asked. "It's me."

"Me who, I have so many boyfriends."

"Very funny, just open the damn door!"

"Okay hold on to your girdle." Then she buzzed him in. He made his way to the second floor. When he got on her floor, he tuned to his right. He took three steps and stopped dead in his tracks. Alice was holding her door opened for him. He couldn't believe what he was looking at. She was wearing a white gold sequin floor length evening gown. Jay just stood there looking at her. "Well, you coming in or what?" Alice asked. He slowly walked to the door. Alice had to step out of his way, so he can go through the door. As he walked into the apartment, he never took his eyes off her.

"Jay, are you okay?" She asked. Jay had a lump in his throat, that he wasn't able to speak. Then these words came out of him. "You're beautiful," he said in a raspy voice. "Well, you're not bad either. Ready?" Alice answered back. "Ready, we should be there by 5:35." Jay said.

When going to pick Alice up the traffic was pretty light, now that it was later, traffic started getting heavy. A trip that would normally take thirty minutes took almost an hour. The parking lot was already starting to fill up. They didn't get to their seats 'til six. The theater was filling up rapidly. Around six thirty the orchestra were tuning up their instruments. Promptly at 7:00 the light in auditoria dimmed. The curtain opened; the opera was beginning. Jay loved to listen to Giovanni sing. Jay was more concerned about the audience. He wanted to see if he can deduct any strange movement from anyone. Everything seemed to be in order. He guessed that he would just have to wait for the end of the show.

At intermission Jay and Alice went to the bar to grab a couple of drinks. Alice got a Neapolitan; Jay ordered a beer. They took their drinks to their seats.

The curtain just started to open as they sat down. Jay decided to relax and take in the rest of the opera. During the performance Giovanni kept taking a glance at Jay. After the curtain went down for the last time, the cast came on this side off the curtain and took their bows. The whole place gave then a standing ovation. The applause and ovation lasted for three curtain calls. During the ovations Giovanni kept looking in Jay's direction. Jay could sense that something was wrong.

Jay waited 'til fifteen minutes, he got up. "Alice I'm going to see Giovanni now, do you want to come or meet me at the bar after I see what the hell's going on," Jay asked. Alice didn't hesitate a second. "Yes, I'll go with you. I haven't met Giovanni yet. So, I guess this is as good of a time as ever. Lead the way, Boss."

Jay and Alice made their way toward the dressing rooms. The dressing rooms were up one floor. Sixteen steps up. All the rooms were on his left. While they looked for Giovanni's room, they were reading all of the names on the doors. Giovanni's room was the last one. Alice was leaning against the railing; Jay went to knock on his door. He made a fist and knocked once. "Hey, maestro you decent. No response. He cocked his arm to knock again, just before his fist made contact with the door, he heard a gunshot from inside of Giovanni's dressing room. Jay pulled his .45 and put his shoulder into the door breaking it in. While Jay went into the room, Alice staid outside of the door to keep people away from the scene.

As Jay entered the room, he sees Giovanni slumped over on his chair, by his dressing table. As he gets closer to Giovanni, he could smell the presents of gunpowder. Jay went up to Giovanni, he noticed that his German Luger that he took of a German Lieutenant when he shot it out of the German's hand as he raised it, ready to shoot Jay in the back of the head. The good Lieutenant thought that he was going to die anyway, so he decided that he would take someone with him.

Giovanni seen the Lieutenant raise his luger. Giovanni whipped out his pistol and shot the gun out of his hand. Jay new it was Giovanni's pistol, because he took it as a souvenir, it had the piece of pistol grip that was missing.

"Alice, call Mike."

"Okay Jay. People are starting to gather by the door, there's also an Army Major out here. He wants to come in. He said that he's the military liaison in charge of the opera tour."

"Send him in."

"Major, you're in charge of the tour. Why?"

"I'm Major Hart, I was assigned to this detail. The tour is visiting many military bases. With the way things are in Europe, with Hitler and Mussolini. When Mussolini made this proposal, Washington thought it to be a little suspicious. So, the White House assigned me the assignment. I've been with this group a few months now. Started in Italy went to India, Australia, Japan and our last stop in Honolulu. These people are no more spies than I am," the Major explained. Jay said, "I know what you mean, if Giovanni was a spy, then I'm the Pope. We can't touch anything until the cops show up." While Jay was at the door, Jay was making mental notes of the room and where everything was. Just then Alice made her way through the crowded hallway.

"Mikes on his way, he said ten minutes." Mike arrived with three squad cars, and six uniforms to control the crowds. Mike was making his way to Giovanni's room he was with two police officers and the coroner. "People, everyone go back to your rooms, NOW!" Mike shouted at all the spectators. Jay, Alice, and Major Hart were waiting for him just inside of the dressing room. Mike asked, "Did anyone hear or see anything?"

"Only heard the gunshot," Jay told him. "Let the coroner do his work, we'll wait out here," said Mike.

After twenty minutes the coroner came out of the room. Mike asked, "well doc, what's the verdict?"

"Well, with all the evidence that I could see, it's a suicide."

"No way," Jay said. I knew him for eighteen years. Giovanni wasn't the type to commit suicide.

While Giovanni was taken to the morgue, Jay and Mike looked around the room. The door that Jay broke down was the only way in or out. The closet door was closed. "Jay, you knew him. Do you think that he's capable of this," asked Mike. "I really doubt it. He had so much, rich, a great baritone, loved around the world. Why would he throw all that away?" Jay asked Mike, Mike do you mind if I stay around for a while, I still want to take a look around. Mike do me a favor, can you take Alice home?" Everyone was gone, back to the hotel. Before the Major left Jay asked, "Major what happens now?"

"I'm not really sure. Giovanni's body would probably be shipped home, by the Italian Consulate. His understudy and cousin Mario will take his place."

After Mike left the Opera House, Jay started to do his own snooping. He checked around his desk, the walls, the next place to look at was the closet. The smell of gun smoke was still present. He opens the closet slowly. He stepped inside. I seemed like the odor was stronger in the closet. He checked the racks of costumes and props. He took his flashlight out to take a look on the floor. Something on the floor catches his eye. When he picked it up, it was a small burnt piece of paper. Jay took a sniff at the paper. There was a real strong gunpowder odor on it. Jay started to check the ceiling. He moved his light slowly the look at ceiling. There was a light with a pull string to turn it on. He did noticed something in the ceiling. He went into the dressing room, took a chair into the closet. He stepped on the chair to get a closer look at the ceiling. He so very lightly ran his hand on the ceiling. Most of the tiles on the ceiling were ten by ten inches, except one. It was twelve by twelve inches.

Pushing the panel up he found out that it was a trapped door.

Jay threw his flashlight up, then lifted himself up. After he made it through the trapped door, he found himself on a catwalk. There was a ten foot later. He also found a piece of a 7" pipe with one side capped. He took a sniff of the pipe. More gunpowder smell and little shards of burnt paper. He looked around with his light. He could only follow the catwalk one way, because Giovanni's room was the last one. He started walking down the catwalk. He noticed that every dressing room had a trap door. "Interesting," Jay thought to himself.

At the end of the catwalk was a set of stairs going down. There was another staircase, it looked like it was going down to the basement. Jay followed the stairs down. He came to a dark hallway; he had his flashlight in his left hand and his .45 in his right hand. At the end of the hallway was a door. The door had a sign on it, BOILER ROOM and JANITOR.

He slowly opened the door. He could feel the heat from the boiler. He found his way to the janitor's desk; it was fairly close to the boiler. He call a few times for the janitor. Jay knew the janitor slept down here some place. He walked past the boiler to another door. Again, he called out to the janitor, nothing. Jay let himself into the room, there was a bed, radio, dresser, and a small bathroom. The only thing that wasn't there was the janitor.

Jay then went back to search the desk. There wasn't anything in the desk. As he started to walk away, he notice a photo underneath a desk bladder. Jay picked the photo up; it was a picture of a military company from the last war. Nothing strange about that, except this was a photo of Germans. Obviously, the janitor was in the German Army. Nothing odd about that. Many Germans immigrated to the U.S.

He looked around once again with his light. Being the boiler was there, there was a coal bunker. He glanced at the coal with his light. A piece of coal looked odd. This piece of coal was a little more shinny then the other coal. Jay went over and picked the piece of coal up and examined it with the lamp by the desk. It was a splatter of fresh blood.

Jay looked around the boiler room. He noticed that the door to the boiler was opened about six inches. He looked around the room. He found a pair of welding goggles. Jay put on a pair of gloves and the goggles. He opened the door to the boiler furnace. He gave out a little gasp. He found the remains of a burning body. His scull still had skin and hair on it.

"Suicide my ass! Something is going on and I'm gonna find out what." Jay said to himself. Mike left two offices at the Opera House just to keep the building secured. Jay told them what he found. "I'll call Mike first thing in the morning to let him know about the corpse." Jay told them as they let him out. It was almost three am, instead of going home he went right to his office. When he got to the office, he took his shoes, the tux, put on other cloths. Lied down on his couch and tried to get sleep. The only thing that he did, was think about tonight's events. He figured if he fell asleep Alice would wake him up when she came to work at 7:00am.

# Chapter Four

7:00am Alice enters the office. She sees Jay on the couch snoring his ass off. She walked over to the windows, this lime instead of letting the shade go, she opened the slowly. The office had four windows. When she lifted the last shade, the bright sun light shined right on Jay.

Jay woke up, focusing his eye with the brightness of the room. Alice put on a pot of coffee. "So, what did you find out," she asked. "I can tell you one thing, it wasn't a suicide, he was murdered," he told her. "I have to call Mike." Jay picks the phone up and dials. "San Francisco P.D. Sargent Ryan, can I help you?"

"Hello Steve, it's Jay. Let me talk to Morris."

"Homicide Lt. Morris."

"Mike it's Jay, I found out a few things."

"Like what," Morris asked. "It wasn't suicide, he was murdered. I'll explain later. We have to keep this quiet for the time being. I want everybody to think he committed suicide. You and me are the only ones that know, except the two cops that let me out. I told them to talk to you before they talk to anyone else. They agreed, they'll only talk to you."

"Okay Jay, what do you have up your sleeve?" The opera has one more performance tonight. Tomorrow the opera company is going on a tour of the city. They leave by train on Tuesday. Tomorrow I'm going to talk to A.J. and ask him if me and Alice can hitch a ride on the train. I'm gonna tell him that I'm from New Jersey and I haven't been home for over four years."

"I don't think that he'll give you a problem. One thing I found out about him. If you two are on a first name basest, he'll do anything for a friend. I wouldn't be surprised if he doesn't pay for everything for you guys. I know you; you're not going because your home sick. You're going to find out who killed him, aren't you?" Well, do you blame me? I own my own detective agency, and besides me I have only one employee. one that has the time for this. Oh, I forgot to tell you, I found a body toasting in the furnace."

"Do you know who it was?"

"I'm pretty sure that it was the janitor. I'll be over tomorrow after I leave A.J.'s and tell you exactly what I think happened."

"Okay Jay see you tomorrow."

"Alice, hold down the fort, I'm on my way to see Mr. Wainsford."

"For what?"

"I'll tell you when I get back. I'm going to ask him something. I'll fill you in when I get back."

"Okay Boss I'm holding down the fort."

"Very funny, I'll be back by lunch. Me and A.J. were supposed to meet for lunch today. I have to cancel lunch and talk to him about something."

"Okay be secretive."

Jay went to see A.J. He arrived on the 12th floor. As he was walking toward the receptionist. "Morning Mr. Jax," she said. "You can go right in. I'll let him know that you're on your way." Thank you, Victoria." Jay thought to himself, "wow, I'm getting first class treatment. It's nice to have friends in high places."

Jay walked into the office. Wainsford immediately rose from his desk. "Jay it's good to see you. I heard what happened to Giovanni, I'm truly sorry."

"A.J., that's why I'm here. Your train that is taking to opera company to New York tomorrow. I'm originally from New Jersey, I was wondering if it would be possible for me and my assistant to hitch a ride on the train? It's been a long time since I've seen my baby sister, baby sister she's in her forties, but Gail will always be my baby sister.

A.J. didn't hesitate for a second. "Jay it would be a pleasure and privilege. I'll call my Yardmaster later this afternoon. I'll even have him hookup my private Pullman Car. If you're going, you might as well go first class. I'll even give you my best cook, and my head porter, they will take extra care of you. Are you investigating why Giovanni committed suicide?"

"No, I really don't want to know. I want to remember him as I did. Me and Alice are just going to go on a vacation."

"That's good, with all you've been through I can understand that." Jay said, "Thank you A.J... "let me know when you're ready to come back to San Francisco, I'll have New York hook my car back up. Might as well come home in first class. "Thank you again A.J., by the way I'm going to have to cancel our lunch date." That's fine, by the way my housekeeper is German. I told her that she can go home to see her family, as long as she comes back. Her name is Dorothia, we just call her Dottie. She'll be sailing on the Manhattan; it's taking the Olympic Team to Berlin. She's been on many of train trips, she goes with Ann and myself when I go on business trips."

Jay left and headed back to his office. When he got back to his office Alice was on the phone. Jay waited till she was off the phone. "Alice, come in hear a minute."

"On my way."

"Do you have anything planned for the next few weeks or so?" He asked her. "What do you have in mind?"

"We are going on vacation."

"Vacation are you serious?"

"I went to talk to Mr. Wainsford, I asked him if we would be able to hitch a ride and see my sister in New Jersey. He thought that we were going to investigate Giovanni's suicide. I told him that this was strictly vacation. I really don't think that he believed me. Nobody knows that were P.I.'s, except for A.J. So, we have that in our favor. So, you go home and pack for at least four weeks. I'll pick you up around 0630. We have to be at the rail yard no later than 0730."

Jay and Alice both left at the same time. Alice went right home, and Jay went to see Mike. He went right up to Mike's office. Jay knocked on Mike's door. "Come on in." Jay opened the door and walked in. "How did you know it was me?" Jay asked. "Ryan called and told me. What's up?"

"Me and Alice are going on a little vacation. Wainsford is letting us hitch a ride to New York, so I can visit my sister."

"Going on vacation, my ass. You're going to find out what's going on."

"Just because you're a detective you think you know me. Well, you do."

"Someone wanted him dead. I'm going to find out why and who. The thing that I have to think about is, why was Mussolini so anxious to send their national opera company on this tour. Mussolini and Hitler are friends. The only one that trust Hitler is the German people and Mussolini. I have a feeling that if there is a war, Germany and Italy will become allies. Don't forget, this is an ITALIAN opera company. We both know that Giovanni loves the United States. I have no idea who these other Italian's are. I think that's why Major Hart is the liaison. I think he's here to keep an eye on them."

Mike asked, "is there anything you want me to do at this end?" Yea, call Chan in Honolulu, ask him if anything weird happened there when the opera was there."

"I can do that. Besides, I haven't talked to Chan since he was in Frisco. Okay Jay, watch your back. Whoever did this won't be too happy that you're on the train."

"You know me Mike, I'm always careful."

"Don't forget Alice will be with you."

"Don't underestimate her, she can take care of herself. Remember last Christmas when she was Christmas shopping when that idiot tried to steal her gifts. Remember what happened to him?"

"That's right I forgot about that. Let see if I remember correctly, as I remember he wound up in the hospital with a broken jaw and sore nut? Maybe she should protect you, instead of the other way around."

"Maybe she will. I'll be in touch along the way."

"Okay I guess I'll see you when you get back." The two men shook hands then Jay started to head for the door. As he did, he turned around to Mike. "Don't forget, no one knows that I'm a P.I."

Jay went back to his office to pick the only piece of luggage that he owned. Then he left for home. He didn't have any more contact with the opera until they went to on board the train.

# Chapter Five

J ay got up about 5:45. Took a shower, dresses and had his morning cup of coffee. At 6:15 there's a knock on the door. "Can't be the cab yet," he thought to himself. He walked over to open the door; he was a bit surprised when he sees who it is. "You ready to go, or what?" Alice asked. "I told you that I would pick you up at 6:30," said Jay. Alice replied, "why wait? The cab driver brought my bags up. Jay looks into the hallway; she had her bags all right. Two large suitcases a makeup case and last but not least her briefcase. "I told you to pack for a few weeks." Alice answered, "a girl has to be prepared." They sat and had some coffee. At 6:25 a car started to hunk the horn. "That must be the cab, if I knew you were coming here, we could have used your cab.

Alice carried her briefcase and the makeup bag. Jay not only carried his one suitcase; he carried her two big suitcases. It wasn't easy. After struggling with Alice's bag, they finally came out the front door. It wasn't a cab, it was Wainsford's driver and his limo. "Let me put your bags in the trunk," said the driver. "Mr. W. decided being you were going first class; you might as well go to the train in first class. My name is Jackson."

"Pleased to me you Jackson. You can call me Jay, and this is Alice."

"We should be at the rail yard in about forty-five minutes, so sit back and enjoy the ride. I know that it's early, but if you like there's a stocked bar. Just push that green button and it will open."

"It's just a little bit early to indulge. We'll just relax."

They arrived at the rail yard at 7:20. Jackson pulled right in front of the Yardmaster's office. Jackson removed their luggage and vanished in seconds. Jay knocked on the office door. A tall skinny man answered the door. "Are you Hector?"

"You must be Mr. Jax plus one," asked Hector. "That's us, I'm Jay and my partner is Alice."

"Follow me and be careful, we have to walk across some tracks.

They been the causes of many sprained and broken ankles. Fifteen years ago, when I started here. On the third week I broke my ankle. I thought there goes my job. Not working for Mr. W. He not only let me keep my job he paid the doctor's bill, that bill had to be at least fifty dollars. During the depression he kept us all working. The train will be the only one that's idling on track seven. The Pullman is all cleaned and stocked. It even has a built- in liqueur cabinet."

As they finally made it to the train, they noticed that it was a long train. At least fourteen cars. They had to walk the whole length of the train. As they were walking, they pass a sleeping car. Major Hart was standing by one of the car doors. "Morning Major," said Jay. "Mr. Jax and Alice, I didn't know that you would be on the train."

"Well Major, I'm originally from New Jersey. A few weeks ago, I met Mr. Wainsford. We became friends. Yesterday I asked him if we would be able to hitch a ride to New York so I can go home and visit my old job and my sister, I haven't been home for close to five years. He said no problem, so here we are."

"Well, welcome aboard. It should be a very boring trip."

"We'll see," added Jay.

They made their way to the end of the train to find the Pullman. "Here it is," Jay said. "Did you use your many years as a seasoned sleuth or is because there ain't anymore cars on the train" Alice said. "Shut up and get on the train," Jay said with a little chuckle. The Pullman didn't have a door, so they had to use the car in front of the Pullman. They use the galley car door.

Jay put the luggage up into the car. Just as fast as he put the luggage in the train, they disappeared just as quick. The porter snatched them up and put them right into their bedrooms. Alice walked up the stairs and made a left into the Pullman, Jay was right behind her.

Alice couldn't believe what the car looked like. When Jay walked into the Pullman Alice had already taken her shoes off. She was gliding along the carpet. She looked like she was ice-skating. Then Jay said, "well, does the car meet your expectations? "Are you kidding, this place is gorgeous! Boy Mr. Wainsford must really like you."

Jay said, "it's not that, he thinks I saved his marriage. Which I didn't, he did all that himself. I just gave him a push. But like they always say, it's good to have friends in high places. He even wants me to call him A.J. I probable already told you that, if I didn't tell you before, I'm telling you now."

"That's funny, I always knew you were losing your memory, or are you just losing you mind," Alice said. "Maybe I am losing my mind, you still work for me." They both started laughing. The porter introduced himself. "Good morning, I'm Isaac. Your porter. Mr. W. Told me to take good care of the Mister and misses." Alice spoke up immediately, "Oh, we're not married. We just work together."

"Sorry Mam, I just thought you were a couple." Alice whispered something in Isaac's ear. Jay was in his bedroom sorting out his cloths. He left his room and asked Isaac, "Isaac I was just wondering, how did you know what bags went to what room?"

"It's easy, the woman always packs too much, and your bag just looked like your Bag," Isaac said with slight grin.

As the train started leaving the rail yard a big fella comes in. "Good morning. My name is Chuma, I'm your traveling chef, from now all the way to New York. Mr. W. told me to make anything your little 'O hearts want, and I mean anything."

"Thank you, Isaac and Chuma. If I need anything, I'll call you." Before Isaac made it to the door, he turned around and said. "By the way, the cabinet against the wall there, isn't just a pretty piece of furniture it's also a fully stocked bar."

"Thank you, Isaac, that's good to know." Jay walked over to the cabinet and opened it up. "Stocked, that's an understatement. There must be a hundred bottles in there, plus beer!" Jay exclaimed. "Care for a drink my dear."

"At eight in the morning, I don't think so." Jay said, "okay, then lunch."

The train was now sliding by San Francisco suburbs and nearing San Jose as the sun burned of the morning fog and beamed earthward. They went back to the easy clickety clack of the wheels and the swaying of the coach when they heard a knock on their door. It was Chuma with some breakfast. "Here's your breakfast," Chuma said. He brought Jay two eggs, bacon and a cup of coffee, Alice had two poached eggs two strips of bacon and a cup of tea.

Later that afternoon, Jay and Alice feasted on a prime rib and a baked potato. Isaac brought them a bottle of Napa Valley red.

Alice dozing off, and Jay's mind was still busy. He gazed absently at the farmlands of Northern California going by as his mind drifted back through the years. He was thinking of the day he met Captain Giovanni Mattola. Jay was a Marine and Giovanni was an officer in the Italian Intelligence Service.

They met two weeks after Lance Corporal Jimmy Willard was killed in a firefight. Jay really didn't like thinking about the war, it always brings back bad memories. His war nightmares were bad enough. He would have his recurring nightmares. It's usually about Lance Corporal Willard. He always blamed himself with his death. The L/CPL was like a son to him. Jimmy had been with Jay for close to five years. They've been in many campaigns. Jimmy was with him during the Mexico unrest, Haiti. He was a good Marine, then his thoughts went to Giovanni. Giovanni was looking for an Italian traitor. Major General Ettore DeCenza. It seemed like this general commanded the fortified defenses in the Alps between Italy and Austria. If he got to the German's, they would be able to take the whole region.

Alice got up from her nap. She walks over to Jay and puts her hand on his shoulder. "Hey Boss, are you okay? It looked like you were in a trance." Jay answered, "I'm fine. I was just thing about France. I was thinking about Willard and Giovanni. Willard was a good kid and Giovanni commanded respect. I never knew that he was an opera singer until he showed up at my wedding, in 1921. Why do people I love keep dying around me?

Alice said, "you have to look at it this way, remember them as the way they were. I'm sure that you and Angela had many good times."

# Chapter Six

"Your right, I have to start living in the present, not the past." "What time do we get to?" Alice asked Jay, "we should be pulling in about 1800." Answered Jay.

Back is San Francisco, Mike had to wait until the boiler cool down. Mike was with about ten cops at the opera house. The boiler was still warm, but it wasn't hot. Two uniforms put on overalls and made their way to the boiler. One thing they had in their favor the remains were right by the door. By time they got into the boiler, the only thing left was bones. Getting rid of any evidence.

Mike had the remains delivered to the morgue, to see if the coroner can figure out how he died, besides burning to a crisp. Mike returned to the coroner after the coroner had the bones for about an hour. "Well Doc, what's the verdict"

"Lieutenant this man was definitely dead before he was barbequed. "How can you tell just by the bones?"

"When a body is burned unless the temp. of the flames are really high. Being that it was a boiler and not a crematory, the boiler wasn't a high heat. There for the skull was in rather good condition. The skull had a distinct knife wound at the back of his skull," the coroner told him. "Okay Doc send the report to me. I'm going to talk to Jay and let him know what you found."

Jay was still wondering about the photo he found in the boiler room. Why kill the janitor? Just before the train pulled into Union Station Major Hart went up to Jay and told him that he was going to investigate and try to find out why Giovanni took his own life.

The train was about five miles from the station when Alice went up to Jay. "I wonder if I would have time to see my sister for a cup of coffee."

"You mean the aspiring actress. How come you didn't try to get into the Hollywood scene?" She said, "I was the practical one in in the family I thought life would be more exciting working for a big-shot private detective famous worldwide."

"No luck with either, huh?" She shook her head sadly. "Afraid not. What are we going to do first.?"

"Tonight, we go to dinner and just keep our eyes opened. Then we'll see if anyone leaves. You take Enzo and I'll shadow Mario. I found out that they had to gain with Giovanni dead."

"Why do you say that?"

"Both Enzo and Mario have the most to gain. What I didn't know is, that Enzo and Mario are Giovanni's cousins. It's like Cane and Able. Except the were brothers. I heard of families that kill one another, for more power in the family, or jealousy. These two men was supposed to idolize him. I can't believe that they would kill Giovanni so they would be able to climb up the latter."

The tour was traveling in first class, and they were staying at the Hotel Coronado. It had a great view of the bay, and the constant swoosh of the surf reminded you of that. Off in the distance, a ship's horn tooted a lonely sound.

While Jay was waiting in the bar for Alice, Major Hart walked by. "Evening Major. How are you enjoying the train ride"

"I didn't mind. It's going to be a long trip, so I better make the best of it. He lit a cigarette, and took a big drag, and said. Well, I'm off for my evening constitutional. See you in the morning.

Just then Alice showed up. "Was that the Major?"

"Yeah," he said that he was going for a walk before he turns in. "What do you think of the Major?" Asked Alice. "I like him. I think that he's a little worried about this suicide. He thinks that the brass is going to blame him for this situation.

Alice said, "No matter how much I think about this case, I still can't figure out why anybody would want to kill Gio when robbery obvious wasn't the motive. Some grudge. Something that happened long ago. What?"

Jay lit up a long slim cigar and said, "come with me. I think I'll raise some snooty noses with this cigar.

They sat out on the terrace by the pool while Jay smoked. Soon Alice said, "Tell you what, Boss. You'll want me fresh as a daisy tomorrow, so, I'm going to go upstairs, sit on my balcony, and have one more room service drink before turning in. I'll see you at breakfast."

Jay nodded and watched her walk off. She was an attractive girl, she was almost six feet tall, blonde hair. And a figure that would stop guys in their tracks. The crack about her going to Hollywood was only half a joke. She was pretty enough. Jay never thought of her romantically. One day when Angela's spirit tells him to move on. But not until then.

Jay decided to go for a walk. San Diego is a Navy town, full of sailors and Marines. He wanted to walk around to see how much San Diego has changed. He was stationed at the Navy Base; he worked as a Military Police Officer. He remembered going to bars to stop fights and unruly military personnel. When Jay was stationed there in 1924, he didn't drink or smoke. He didn't start any vices at that time. He started after Angela died.

He walked into a bar just to have one drink. The place was a little rowdy, but not like it was when he was an M.P. There were a couple of M.P.'s in the bar making sure that no one was misbehaving. All of a sudden, an M.P. comes up to him and says, "Master Gunnery Sargent Jax. Haven't seen you since 1924. What have you been up to?" Jay looked at him like a deer would look at headlights coming down the road. Then the M.P. said, "it's me. Corporal Miller I worked for you two years as an M.P." Then Jay's memory came back. "Corporal Pete Miller!"

"It's not corporal anymore. Staff Sargent Miller. I'm catching up to your rank. So, what brings you to San Diego?"

"Well, I'm originally from Jersey. I know the owner of the railroad, so I'm hitching a ride to New York. Me and my associate are on the same train that the opera is on."

"I heard that the opera was coming to base. I never been to an opera."

"You'll like it, the music is great, and the performers are excellent. Do you remember talking about my Italian friend, Giovanni?"

"I remember M/Gunnery Sargent. You could tell some good stories."

"Don't believe everything you hear. Well, Giovanni was the star of the opera. He passed away in San Francisco. I decided that I have to get out of town for a while, so I'm going home for a week or two."

"What about your work in San Fran, you are working aren't you?"

"That's what's good about my job. I'm my own boss. I own the Jax Detective Agency. I cleared all my schedule."

"Master Gunnery Sargent it was nice seeing you again."

"A friend once told me that, we are friends, so call my Jay, or Mister Jax. Only kidding about the Mister."

Jay left the bar at 0015 (12:15pm). He wasn't drunk, but he was feeling good. He was only a few blocks from the hotel, so he decided to walk. He hadn't walked two blocks when it happened.

He was passing a dark alley. He knows better than to walk to close to an alley, but he didn't think that anything would happen.

He was hit like a bolt of lightning. The assailant that hit him from behind grabbed him around the arms, while the second mugger went to stab Jay in the stomach. Jay took all of his strength and spun himself and the assailant around just before he got stuck. When he did the knife found its way into the side of the one that was holding him. You could hear the one that just got stabbed yelled out in pain. Then Jay saw the knife headed for him again. Jay brought his right foot up and knocked the knife from his hand. The one who was stabbed came at Jay, his knife wound wasn't that bad. He gave Jay a right cross hitting him in his right cheek. This punch made him a little wobbly. Jay came to his senses quick. Now they both rushed him. Jay was against a wall. The knife was picked up, Jay saw the knife coming towards him, he took his right leg and went for the one with the knife, he kicked the knife wielding thug and kicked him in the nuts. Dropping the knife, the second thug got lucky and gave Jay another right cross. Jay recovered quick. Giving the thug a left cross then a right uppercut. It looked like they had enough and made their way back down the alley. Jay was going to chase them down the alley, the one that was stabbed left a really good blood trail to follow, but thought better of it, he didn't know what was down the alley waiting for him. Jay collected his thoughts, after about ten-minutes he saw a cab approaching, and he waved it down. Before he got into the cab, he picked the knife up.

When he got back to the hotel the bar was closed, so he went back to his room to nursing his injuries. It was almost 2:00am when he finally got to sleep.

He couldn't shake the thought that these guys were in someone's military. He examined the knife. To his astonishment, the knife was a German trench knife. He knew that many G.I.'s bought German knives home. He also realized that Germany still used those knives.

Jay knocked on Alice's door. Alice opened the door and asked, "what the hell happened to you?"

"I'll tell you at breakfast, let' go."

They grabbed a booth in the restaurant. They ordered. Just as Jay was starting to tell Alice about last night, Major Hart showed up. Jay didn't want to tell Hart what happened, as far as anyone knew is that they were on vacation.

"What happened to you?" Hart asked. Jay didn't hesitate with an answer. "I have a bad habit, ever since I got back from France, I have a bad habit of falling out of bed. Use to scare my wife half to death. I have been seeing doctors."

"Just for falling out of bed?" The Major asked. "Not only for falling out of bed, but I also walk in my sleep once and a while, but the main thing is for my nightmares," Jay said. "Boy I thought that, that stuff only happened to me," the Major added. Jay continued, "That's what happened, I fell out of bed, not once but twice. It's embarrassing. A grown man falling out of bed, like a two-year-old. It's funny I haven't fallen out of bed for a few years. Don't know what brought this on," Jay added.

Major Hart ordered breakfast. Jay and Alice started talking about Jersey. Jay was talking about his home and his sister. Alice was wondering if she would like it in New Jersey. Don't forget Alice has never been out of California.

Jay asked Hart, "What time do we leave for the Navy Yard?"

"The show starts at 1900, so we'll be leaving at 1700. This morning the cast and members of the opera company are going on a walking tour through San Diego, they're going to be divided up into six groups. That way they can do some shopping if they choose to. They'll be taken downtown by buses, there will be six local guides."

"Are you going with them?" Jay asked. "Yes, I'll be tagging along.

The only one that's not going is Mario, he's a little under the weather." The Major added. "What are you and Alice going to be doing today?"

"I really don't know, I guess we'll just hang around here. So, we haven't made any plans for today."

After the tour started Jay and Alice were sitting in the lobby, drinking coffee and reading the newspapers. The tour was supposed to be done at 1500. (3:00pm) It was about 1100 when they saw Mario leave the hotel. "Under the weather my ass!" Alice staid in the hotel. Jay made his way outside, just as Mario got into a cab. Jay flagged the next cab in line. Jay got in and told the driver, "follow that cab."

"You got it boss," said the cabby. After following for a while Jay asked, "where do you think he's headed for?"

"It looks like he's headed for the Naval Base," answered the cabby. They were still following him when Mario's cab turned into the Naval Base. Jay watched Mario hand the sentry a piece of paper, the sentry waved him in.

The cab driver asked, "so, what do you want me to do?"

"Follow him." As the cab pulled up to the sentry, Jay never took his eyes off of Mario's cab. At the gate, a Marine sentry approached the cab. "ID sir." Jay showed him his Marine ID. "Okay Master Gunnery Sargent you can go." Jay was at the main gate for only forty seconds. When he didn't see the cab anymore, he asked the sentry, "that cab that came in just before we did, where did he go?"

"I believe he was going to the officers mess."

"Thank you, Sargent."

Jay knew were the officers mess was, so he directed the cab to the officers mess. Jay entered the building. At the desk in the lobby was a Master Chief. "Can I help you sir?" Jay took out his ID and handed it to the Master Chief. "Master Gunny. You do know that this is the officer's mess."

"I was an MP here in 1922. I'm just looking for a friend of mine. He's an Italian, he's in the show tonight. Have you seen him?"

"Sorry Gunny, you're the first civilian that I've seen today."

"Thank you, Chief."

Jay returned to his cab. "Where now?"

"Just take me back to the hotel." So, the cab headed back to the hotel. As they were driving through downtown, they pasted some of the opera crew finishing up their tour.

When Jay got back to the hotel, Alice already went back to her room. Jay entered his room. First thing that he does is go to the adjoining room door and knocked. In a matter of seconds Alice opened the door.

"Well Boss. Did you find out anything?"

"The only thing that I did find out was, I don't tail as good as I use too. He went to the Naval Base. The sentry just waved him through. Then I lost him."

"Some detective you are," Alice said with a slight giggle. "It must be my old age. I guess we're going to wait until tonight's show. Let's go get some dinner."

After dinner, they went to the lounge to have a few drinks. They sat in a corner booth. Jay had his back to the wall, that way he could scope out the whole bar. He does that all the time. It makes him feel safe. He knows that nothing was going to happen, but it's better to be safe than sorry.

After a few drinks they went back up to their rooms. They had to get ready for tonight's show.

# Chapter Seven

At ten to seven they made their way to the lobby; they couldn't afford to miss the buses. When they got to the lobby the whole cast, crew and Major Hart were already in the lobby. "Evening Major"

"Jay, Alice. Are you ready for tonight's show?" The Major asked. "As ready as I can be."

Instead of taking the bus, Jay decided to take a cab. Jay, Alice, and Major Hart all took the same cab. Their cab got to the base and the theater area before the buses. So, they decided to take a look around the area. Major Hart went back to the stage area. The stage was only about fifty yards from the docks. As they were walking around two Navy sentries approached them. It wasn't dark yet, but the sun was getting low in the sky, glowing a bright orange.

"Halt who goes there?" One sentry said as he walked towards them. Jay had no password, so he had to think quick. "Master Gunnery Sargent retired Jay Jax with the opera."

"Don't move. Let's see some ID." Jay reached into his pocket, and slowly produce his military ID. While one sentry had his rifle pointed at Jay. The sentry looked at his ID, looked back at Jay, then back to the ID. Then he handed it back to Jay. "Sorry sir you can go."

"Don't be sorry, that's your job and the sign of a good sailor."

It was getting close to curtain time, so Jay and Alice decided to return to the stage. Jay, Alice, and Major Hart had reserved seats. "Hope you don't mind, but I called the X.O. Captain Roberts, and asked if he could hold three chairs for us," the Major told them. "Well Major that's using your head. Now we don't have to stand for three hours.

The show started promptly at 1900. "7:00pm" Jay and Alice took their seats. The Major sat down, except he was constantly getting up and down. Jay said to Alice, "boy the Major takes his job seriously. He's always doing something, plus I think that he's still upset and worried about Giovanni's suicide. I told the Major that he can't blame himself. I think he believes that it was his fault."

"We only have 'til New York to find out what happened. Do you trust the Italians?" Alice asked. "I really don't know. With what's going on in Europe. There's talk that Mussolini is making deals with Hitler. Who knows, someday everyone associated with this opera, may wind up being our enemies." Alice answered back, "Let's not worry about that now, let's just relax and enjoy the show."

The intermission was about fifteen minutes away. The intermission was a half hour. Jay and Alice returned to their seats. During intermission they just walked around by the docks, they stopped for a couple of minutes and had a little talk with the sentries that challenged them earlier. Jay was telling them about the time he was stationed at the Navy Yard. He told them about the times that he went into town and busted many drunk sailors and Marines.

After talking to the sentries, they made it back to the stands. They didn't sit in the reserve seats that Major Hart got for them. This time they went to the top row, that way they would be able to see everyone. Especially Mario and Enzo. Mario disappeared for around fifteen minutes. They didn't notice which way he left. Finally, Mario entered the stage.

Back on the docks you can see the worker that was working in the warehouse. In the distance there's a dark figure walking towards the warehouse worker. When they were only a few feet apart. The dark figure said to the worker. "Nice evening tonight, don't you agree?"

"I agree, except it's a little cool," said the worker.

"Sargent, do you have anything for me?" Asked the dark figure. "Yes, I have many things. Everything that I been acquiring over the past year, ever since I heard about the operation. I have maps of the Navy Yard, copies and blueprints on two aircraft carriers, the location where the submarine are docked at."

"Good the Fuhrer would be pleased. I won't be surprised if you get a medal and promotion. Go back to your duties, the sentries should be making their rounds shortly." The warehouse worker turned around to go back to the warehouse. When the dark figure took his left hand and grabbed the worker putting his hand over the worker's mouth. With his right hand he trust a trench knife and stabbed him in the back of his neck and twisted the knife to the right. Killing him instantly. He took the corpse and pushed him into the bay. This took no more than five minutes. The figure turned and walked back through the darkness whence he came.

The opera was about twenty-minutes from final curtain. The sentries were making their rounds on the docks. When one of them sees someone in the water. "HALT who goes there," yelled the senior sentry. Nothing, he challenged three more times. "Answer, or we will open fire. When the sentries didn't get a response, they started shooting at the figure in the water.

The shots were heard by everyone at the opera. The C.O. of the base ran toward the sounds of the gunfire. Hart jumped up and started heading to the shots. Jay and Alice were right behind him. All total about twenty people found their way to the dock. Captain Roberts was on the scene. The Captain asked the sentries. "Chief what's going on, what were you shooting at?"

"We were making our rounds when we saw someone or something in the water, we challenged three or four times. When we didn't get a response, we opened fire. I'm saying that we must have hit him at least eight times." When they looked at the water, there was definitely a body in the water.

Captain Roberts said, "I need two volunteers to retrieve the body." The sentries spoke up first. "Well Captain, being we shot him, we volunteer." There was a rowboat tied up about fifteen yards away from them. While the sentries went to pick up the body, Captain said to the crowd, "everyone please return to your seats. Everyone leave except the sentries, MP's and SP's. Major you can stay. Jay and Alice turned to go back to their seats, when Captain Roberts called "Master Gunnery Sargent front and center."

Jay and Alice started to walk back where the Captain was. "I'm confused, how do you know me?" Jay asked.

"You don't remember me?"

"I know that I'm getting old, I guess my memories going."

"It was 1920 you were an MP. I was an awkward Lt. J G, Lieutenant Roberts."

"Sure, I remember now. Didn't I arrest you once in town?"

"Gunny I would rather forget that if you don't mind. If you know what I mean."

"Forget? Forget what? I have no idea what you're talking about."

"So, Gunny how have you been?" Asked the Captain. "I live in San Francisco as a consultant."

"If I remember correctly, weren't you from New Jersey. I remember when you and your wife lived at the NCO housing. If I'm not mistaken your wife's name is Angela. How she doing?" Jay started to get a little teary eyed. "My wife was murdered during a bank robbery."

"I'm sorry Gunny, I had no idea. I am so sorry."

"That's okay, that was eight years ago. Do you remember Staff Sargent Mike Morris?"

"Yes, I remember Mike. How is he?"

"He's doing good. He's a Lieutenant on the San Francisco Police Department. He's married with three kids, two girls and a boy."

"That's great, well let's get back to the present. Master Chief take the body to Doctor Fosters. Tell him to start the autopsy. We'll be there in a little bit."

"Captain, it's after 2200, he's probably sleeping."

"Then wake him up!"

"Yes Sir."

The opera did finish the opera. Like Giovanni said, "The Show Must GO ON." Captain Roberts, two SP's, two Marine MP's, Jay, Major Hart and the sentries made their way to the doctor's office. The doctor was deep into the autopsy. "Well Doc, did you find anything?"

"I know one thing; this man was dead before he wounded in the bay."

"Explain."

"He was shot six times, but the bullets didn't kill him. He was stabbed in the back of his neck; the blade went right into his brain killing him instantly. Whoever did this knew what he was doing. Then he was thrown in the water."

"How can, you be sure."

"Even though he was shot. If he were shot and alive in the water, there would be water in his lungs."

We have another murder. What the hell's going on. Alice left with the opera back to the hotel. After discussing the events that just took place. It was now past 2300. Jay and the Major took a cab back to the hotel. On the way home they discussed the murder. The Major said, "if I didn't know any better, I'd say that this opera was cursed."

"I believe that it's a little more than being jinxed or cursed. It's all got something to do with Giovanni's suicide. But what?" The Major asked, "we started the tour in Italy, India to entertain the British troops, Australian troops, New Zealand, Japan, Hawaii, then San Francisco. Everything went off without a hitch. I just can't figure what's happening."

Jay told the Major, "I'm glad that me and Alice are on vacation. To tell you the truth I really don't want to know what or who he was into. I feel for you Major. I can't even imagine what's going through you mind. Are you still investigating on the train? I believe we have a killer in our mist."

"Jay, I think you're right, but who is it?" Jay replied, "well Major you have to find out by New York. Being you're going with them on The Manhattan you have until Berlin to find the killer. I would help, but we're on vacation."

When they arrived at the hotel they decided to go into the bar and have a few. After two drinks the Major decided to go up to his. Jay got up and went to the house phone to call Alice. Alice answered right away, "Hello."

"It's Jay, want to meet in the bar?"

"Not tonight, I'm just lounging on the balcony taking in the cool ocean breeze."

"Okay, what if I bring the bar to you?" Alice said, "that would be fine. I never had a bar come to me before." Jay goes into his room, then he knocked on Alice's adjoining room door.

A voice came from behind the door. "Who is it?"

"Very funny, just open the door!"

"Some detective you are. Have you forgotten anything?"

"What!"

"We never lock our room doors. As long as you knock before barging in. A girl has to be decent." Jay walked into Alice's room with two drinks for Alice. He had two beers tucked away in jacket pocket.

Jay walked onto the balcony and put her drinks on the table. 'So, what happened after I left?" She asked. After we fished body out of the water. they took the body to the doctor's office. He said that the bullets didn't kill him, he was stabbed then thrown into the water."

"What the hell's going on?" She asked. "Well, here's the kicker. The guy that the sentries shot. He was the guy working in that warehouse we passed."

"The plot thickens," she replied. "Ready for this? His name was Kurt, a German name if I ever heard one. They went back to small talk. Jay said goodnight then went back to his room.

# Chapter Eight

O600 Came early. Alice knocked on Jay's door. "You decent boss?"

"Come on in" Alice asked, "Ready for some breakfast?"

"Can't start the day without my morning cup coffee." As they were getting in the elevator, Major Hart put his hand in the closing doors, keeping the door opened. "Morning Jay and Alice. Ready to get back on the train?"

"Eat first, train second," replied Jay.

When they entered the dining room. It seemed like the whole opera company were already eating. So, Jay, Alice and the Major all sat together. Jay asked the Major, "so, Major what unit were you with in France?"

"I was with the 119th Field Artillery Brigade in Prement. About twenty miles from Belleau Woods and you."

"I was with the 3rd battalion, 5th Marines. Spent most of our time at Belleau Woods. I was one of six Marine Snipers."

"Where and when did you meet Giovanni?"

"That's a long story. He was with an Italian intelligence unit. I was just looking through my scope, nine hundred yards I noticed two targets. It looked a little odd. One target made the other kneel down. I finally figured out what was happening, the Kraut was about to execute the man on his knees. I had to make a split-second decision, even if the man that was about to be executed was a deserter. Nobody should be executed. So, I shot the one that was about to do the executing. I got him in his neck. I didn't want to rush over to him, just in case he had company. It was only me and my spotter. I waited for about a half hour before I made my way to the man lying on the ground. I was fairly sure the man was still alive. My spotter Lance Corporal Willard kept me covered. When I got to the man, he was laying on his side with his eyes closed. I kind of thought that it was funny. I said to myself, "if this guy is playing dead, he's doing a pretty bad job at it." He was moving a little, plus I saw him breathing. I poked at him with my rifle. He tried not to move. Then I said, "are you going to lie there all day, or do you want to get out of here." He answered back in an Italian accent.

"You German?"

"Do I sound German? Let's get out of here before his friends come back. My spotter has use covered."

"We got back to Willard. That's when he told me his story. He was looking for an Italian Major General Ettore DeCenza. He was one of the commanders in the Alps between Italy and Austria. The one German captured him and was going to execute him for being a spy. Luckily, he was separated from his unit. The rest is history, told you it was a long story.

"I can see why you two were such good friends."

"Yes, I did save his life. He stayed with use for about a week. We met up with a patrol, which was Sargent Mike Morris."

"The cop in San Francisco?"

"One and the same," said Jay. "I not only saved his life, but he also wound up saving my life. On the way back to headquarters we hooked horns with a German Patrol. They took cover at an old farmhouse. Some went behind a wall, and three went into the farmhouse. We had to be careful, the ones in the farmhouse had a better view on us."

"We were in a good location, we had good concealment. A Corporal was wounded in his leg. Lance Corporal Willard was trying to get a better position. We kept up cover fire. Then I saw Willard go down. He was shot twice. In the hip and one behind his left ear, he was dead. That's when we started to lob mortars at them. One hit the roof of the farmhouse taking care of the three. After fifteen minutes everything got eerily quiet. We made our way to the wall. Morris lob a grenade over the wall.

"All the German's were down, some wounded and some dead. We made our way to the farmhouse and through in two grenades. Then we started to see who was dead and who was wounded. Giovanni was in front of the farmhouse, his back to the front door. I was facing him with my back to the wall. All of a sudden Giovanni pulled his pistol and shot once. It seemed that this Kraut Lieutenant was playing dead, he raised his Luger and was aiming at the back of my head. He shot the good Lieutenants Luger out of his hand. Didn't hit the Lieutenant, he hit the butt of his pistol, knocking a piece of butt out. Good shot. That's how we met."

Alice was sitting there taking in the story, Jay never told her how they became friends. They finished their breakfast, then they got on the buses to go to the station. When they got to the station, the baggage handlers were putting their luggage, props, and costumes into the baggage car.

As soon as they entered the Pullman Car, Isaac and Chuma was there to greet them back. Isaac spoke first, "welcome back, like before if you need anything just call me. I restocked the bar." Now Chums spoke, "I restocked the kitchen, with meat, vegetables and fruit. Whatever you need, we probably have it."

"Thank you. Believe me if we need anything, we'll let you know." Jay and Alice settled down for the two-day trip to El Paso.

# Chapter Nine

Jay and Alice alternately dozed and watched the southern dessert roll by in a panoramic vista that supplied wonders regularly. The land changed often. From saw tooth mountain ridges, to barren open dessert, to sequoia and sage dotted sand. The trip from San Diego to El Paso was about nine hundred miles. They had two whole days to try and figure what they're missing.

There was a knock on their door. Alice answered to door. It was Dottie, Wainsford maid. "Dottie, we haven't seen you this whole trip. What have you been doing?" Asked Alice. "This might be vacation to You's, but for me I have to keep busy. While you are off train I still work. I clean your rooms. Wash sheets, polish furniture, vacuumed carpet and anything else I find."

"Thank you, Dottie, will you join us for dinner tonight?"

"I think I get in trouble."

"None sense. I don't think Mr. Wainsford would mind. Well, if you change your mind, let Isaac know."

"I will sir." Dottie left, and Jay and Alice went back to their sightseeing mode.

The gentle swaying and the clickety clacking, while it was conducive to thinking, could also easily lull the lazy mind into frequent slumber.

Jay had a mental list of the people he would like to speak to, hopefully before they reach El Paso. Giovanni has two cousins in the opera and they both were understudies, Mario De Luca, and Enzo Baresi. Jay was thinking about putting them at the top of his suspect list. His co-star Donatella Stancati. Not that he considered her as a suspect. She really didn't have anything to gain if Giovanni died. Not like Mario and Enzo. Who had everything to gain, but killing their cousin, Jay just didn't know? Mario stopped by just after lunch. He was an affable guy who, it was soon obvious, adored and admired Giovanni. Jay decided to go seeDonatella Stancati, to see if she can put a little more light on Giovanni. Jay knocked on Donatella's door. He heard a soft voice coming from the other side of the door, "who is it?"

"It's Jay Giovanni's friend."

"Come in." Jay entered the small room. The rooms decor, a twin bed, and a small chest of draws near the door. "I hate to intrude; I was wondering if you can tell me a little more about Giovanni? Like what he was like when not performing."

"Giovanni was great baritone, all of us will miss him. Mario and I will be doing our best to uphold Giovanni's memory. There's really nothing else to say. Oh, I did forget to tell you, when we perform in Washington, President Roosevelt, General Holcomb, I believe he's the Commander of your Marine people."

"Commandant of the Marine Corps." Jay explained to her. "Does the Major know this?"

"Yes, he's the one that told us."

"I'm sure you miss him, Signora, we all miss him. I've known him for eighteen years, but I really don't know anything about him."

"I'm sorry Signor Jax that I can't help you anymore."

"Jay, you can call me Jay. Nonsense, you've been a great help."

As Jay left, he realized that he learned nothing from her. As the miles and the landscape ticked by, the desert sequoia cactus evolved to saw- tooth mountain ranges to barren country with stark rock formations.

When Jay returned to the Pullman, Alice had to unfold her scrunched long legs and sit up from her nap while Jay went to the washroom to wash up and revive himself from his own stuporous doze.

Later that afternoon, Jay and Alice were talking about the case. Jay often used her as a sounding board for his ideas. Not that he had any at that moment, but it was always better to brainstorm with another person.

Jay said, "if I had my board up in the office, I would list the things that have happened so far. Try to figure out which are related, and which are pure coincidence."

Alice said, "start with Gio's note about the world tour."

"Yeah, the put down that he must have been suspicious of something since he wanted to meet after the show."

Alice thought that over. "I think we don't have anything with that, Jay.

Wouldn't Gio want to see you after the show anyway?"

Jay thought about that. "Yeah, to some degree, but why was he Killed before we had the meeting?"

"I think you have put that down as borderline coincidence?" Jay lapsed deep in thought. "Well, how about the German we found in the furnace?"

"Didn't many Germans immigrate to the U.S. After the war?" Jay sat up. "Hey. What did Einstein say about coincidence?" Alice shook her head. Jay said, "he said, coincidence is God's way of remaining anonymous."

Alice asked, "did Einstein really say that?" Jay answered, "I don't know, I never met the man." Many more miles clacked by, and the two sat staring at the window.

Jay asked Alice, "come up with anything?" Alice said, "I'm just looking at the scenery."

And that's why I pay you the big bucks. She smiled, "That and I have great legs."

This repartee was part of their chemistry. Often times, their brainstorming seemed like it was hitting a blank wall and then something would pop.

Alice asked, "do you see any common thread here?"

"No, I can't say that I do. Unless of course, you want to consider that photo of German soldiers together during the war."

"Hmm. That's a pretty thin part of the thread. I know you think you see something German here. Something to do with the past."

They looked at each other for some confirmation, but none came. She added, "but frankly, I don't see any of that."

"What about the muggers that attacked me? They weren't the run of the mill muggers. These guys were in good shape, and he knew hand-to-hand combat."

"Lots of guys know hand-to-hand combat. That doesn't really prove anything unless you're going to stick your mind so deep into your theory. "You weren't the only one who was in the service."

He thought about that for a while. "I guess you're right. It's too early in the investigation to get married to any theory. Not with what we have for evidence. Which is nothing."

Her eyes narrowed as she watched his expression. She knew him well enough to know that he hadn't abandoned the idea that the murder had its roots somewhere in the past and had something to do with the war.

They were sitting in their train car nursing after dinner drinks. Alice recognized that faraway look in his eye. "So, I didn't have any luck dissuading you about your theory?"

"Why do you say that?"

"I can see the wheels turning."

"I'm just thinking about it all. Like that dock worker in Pearl Harbor. Hawaii isn't a hotbed of crime these days, so, a murder doesn't go unnoticed."

"Didn't you say that it was investigated as an accidental drowning until they found the knife wound in the back of his neck?"

"Yeah, that's right, but the other thing is, he was Japanese?"

Alice said flatly, "aren't there lots of Japanese in Hawaii these days?"

"I got a telegram when we were in San Diego."

"From?"

"Mike, he said that the victim, it turns out, was a Japanese national. That means that his home is in Japan. He's in Hawaii working on a pineapple farm. Mike said that he picks pineapples for a few months, then goes back to Japan, and someone takes his place for a few months."

"I hate to belabor the theme, but the Japanese counterpart of the growing fascist movement in Europe." Alice waited patiently for the explanation. "Lots of people in this country say the winds of war are blowing our way, and the German's, Japan and Italy are in on it."

"But wasn't Japan and Italy on our side in the war," she asked.

"The world is changing fast. The fascist movements are designed for a powerful group to oppose the U.S. From both shores."

Alice didn't look convinced. "Well, that's an interesting political theory, Jay, but what's it got to do with Giovanni's murder?"

"I don't know, Alice. All I know is that my instincts keep Draggin' me back to France."

Alice lowered her eyes. "Jay, you might be right. Your instincts and your gut feelings have solved many of our cases, so I guess I'll relinquish to you."

Jay said, "no I don't want that, Alice. I need another point of view and a new prospective. I may be of on a wild goose chase. All I have is a lot of unfounded theories that somehow involves the past. No, please keep your own ideas. Don't necessarily go along with me. I don't need a yes man, or woman, I should say. I need an independent thinker. Like the mugging. My preconceived theory is already leading me to a conclusion that might be all wrong. Don't you agree? What you said may be more in line. Lots of guys know how to fight. Especially, when half the men in this country are riding the rails as vagabonds. They'd have to learn to fight just to take care of themselves."

"What blows my ideas all to hell is that I'm sure Giovanni had nothing to do with what's happening in the world. Him and me had our war. I'm still fighting mine on the streets of San Francisco, but Gio had become a world-renowned opera singer. I'm sure that's what he was best at. Why would anyone want him dead? That's what I have to keep on my mind. There's some logical reason why he was murdered, and if you're right, it has nothing to do with the past."

Alice said, "in any event, Mike will be a valuable asset in his spot on the police department. He's able to use channels of information that, as Private Eyes, we wouldn't. You never did tell me how you met Mike.

"We go way back. He joined the Corps after I did, even though he was older. I was sixteen. we met in the Dominica Republic. He was a private and I was a Lance/Corporal. When we went to the Philippines, I was a corporal, and he was a Lance/Corporal. After I made corporal,

I went to sniper school. Once and awhile, he'd be my spotter. After the war he went to San Francisco, he eventually became a police lieutenant. I became a cop in Woodbridge New Jersey. When Mike heard that Angela died, Mike sent me a letter with his condolences and asked me if I would consider coming to San Francisco and work with him on the police department. So' I got on a train, joined the San Francisco police Department eventually I became a Sargent. We were involved with a Canadian bootlegger back in 1930. Eventually, we cornered him unloading a shipment of booze, and there was a shootout. I was hit in the right shoulder, knee and the one that almost ended it for me. I was hit in the upper right side of my chest, collapsing my lung. Mike killed the bootlegger when he was about to finish me off."

"Wow that must have involved some serious hospital time."

"I was in the hospital almost a year. I thought that I would go nuts."

"That's what ended your police career?"

"Yep. The only thing that I was good as, was a cop. So, I had to find something at which I was good. That's when I became a P.I. You know how close me, and Mike are. Since the Corps we've been the best of friends. Also, he never lets me forget that he saved my life. I remember saving his life a few times when we were in the Corps. If there's a case that's going nowhere, he calls me, I don't know why I'm telling you that, you know that he calls me when he needs help. He sticks his head out every time I give him a hand. One thing about police departments, Private Eyes aren't there favorite institution."

Alice shook her head. "But that won't come between you guys?"

Jay grinned. "Not even a little. The S.F.P.D. tolerates me. After all I was a cop here."

# Chapter Ten

At 0300 Jay decided to take a stroll to the baggage car. He was going to see if he would be able to search some luggage, maybe he would be able to find out something. It seemed like everyone was asleep, so he walked slowly through the cars. He was swaying side to side with every step he took.

He got to the baggage car, opened the door, trying to be as quiet as he could. It was pitch black in the car. Jay didn't want to turn any lights on. He didn't want to advertise his presents, so he used his flashlight. He wanted to search Enzo's trunk first. All the trunks were locked. Jay thought that they would be. Jay removed his lock picking kit.

He was about to get Enzo's trunk unlocked, when all of a sudden, he hears a pop. He knew immediately, it was a silencer. A round hit the floor in front of him. Jay pulls his .45 and caned the flashlight. Jay ducked behind the pile of trunks. Whoever the shooter is it looked like he was trying to avoid the luggage. Another round whizzed past his right ear. Jay didn't want to fire back, because if he missed it was possible, he might hit someone in the sleeping cars. So, Jay was keeping as low as he could. Jay could see a silhouette by the door. Three more shots went over Jays head. Then it got eerily quiet. Jay didn't want to head for the door, until he knew the gunman was gone. Jay heard the door close. Jay started towards the door. It looked like whoever the shooter was, he's gone now. When he got to the door it was locked. Luckily, the doorknob had keyholes on both sides of the door. He picked the lock and let himself out. As he walked through the train, he checked every compartment to see if anyone was stirring. Everything was quiet.

Jay finally made his way back to the Pullman. He went right to the liquor cabinet. He grabbed a bottle of Jack, sat at the table and poured himself a double. Now he knew someone was starting to get nervous. It takes balls to try and kill someone on a train. More than likely if he were killed, the assassin would through him off the train.

It was now 0415. He decided to go back to bed. Before he went to sleep, he put the bottle of Jack, and leaned it up against the door, so if anyone came in, he would hear the bottle fall, giving him time to react.

At 0730 he heard the bottle fall over. He didn't know what time it was. He jumped to his feet and cautiously made his way out of his room. He looked at the dining room table. It was Isaac setting the table for breakfast.

"Morning, Mister Jax."

"Morning Isaac. I told you to drop the mister and call me Jay."

At that moment Alice came staggering out of her room. "Morning guys. Isaac would it be possible to bring me a cup of coffee. After my coffee I'll be fine. So, Jay, I heard you come in last night. Where'd you go?"

"I'll tell you after breakfast. You might find this interesting; it has something to do with Giovanni."

So, after breakfast, Jay told her the story. "I went to the baggage car, as soon as I started to unlock Enzo's trunk, someone started taking shots at me. I saw whoever it was, but I only saw the silhouette, so I couldn't see a face. He shot about six rounds at me."

"Well, at least now we know the killer is definitely on the train. I didn't hear any gunfire."

"Whoever it was, used a silencer. I never heard a silencer that was as quiet as that one was. It made a dull popping sound. I barely heard it. I wasn't about to return fire. I was afraid that I might hit someone that was sleeping. I hope that whoever it was didn't know that it was me they were shooting at. Major Hart was doing the investigating, maybe they thought that they were shooting at the Major. As far as anyone knows we're on vacation."

"Are you going to tell the Major what happened?" Alice asked.

"No, I'm not going to mention it to anyone. If the shooter thought that they were shooting at the Major, I don't want to let anyone know that it was me."

"It looks like we're going to have to watch our backs. I'm going to take a walk." She said.

"Be careful, you do have you .38 with you?"

"Always, I never go anywhere without it."

"Good girl just be careful. I don't want to lose you know that I made you a partner."

"Jay, don't worry, you know that I can take care of myself. See you in about an hour."

Then Alice left the Pullman.

# Chapter Eleven

Alice decided to do a little snooping on her own. She was going to the whole cast in the opera and just start up a casual conversation. The cast might open up if they talked to a woman. Her first stop was Donatella. Alice knocked on her door. "Who is it?" A voice came from inside the room. It's Alice Jay's associate."

"Please come in." Alice opened the door slowly. "How can I help you?" She asked. Alice replied, "just wanted to talk, we haven't talked since we got on the train. I'd like to find out what kind of person Giovanni was."

"Giovanni was a hell of a baritone; he did have one fault."

"And that is?"

"He liked the ladies. He really didn't care whose lady, if he wanted her, he got her. "Anyone I know?"

"Well, there was Enzo."

"What happened?"

"In 1924 Giovanni had an affair with his wife. That lasted for almost a year. It ended when he got tired of her. Then he had another in his sights."

"Go on."

"In 1926 he had another affair with Mario's wife."

"Interesting, so he had an affair with his two cousins' wives. Why didn't Mario and Enzo do anything?"

"Giovanni is...or was their cousin."

"Boy is Jay going to have a rude awakening." Alice thought to herself. "Well, thank you Donatella, it was a pleasure talking to you."

"One more thing, Giovanni came up to me about one year ago and propositioned me."

"What did you do?" Alice asked her. "I slapped him if the face as hard as I could."

"Good for you girl."

"That's why he only talked to me when he had to." Donatella told her. "Well thank you Donatella. You made things a little clearer."

Alice though that there was no reason to talk to anyone else, she got an ear full-from Donatella. When Alice got back to the Pullman Jay wasn't there. Jay was at the bar talking with the Major. "So, your family owns a farm. Where's the farm?" Jay asked the Major. "About fifty miles north of Milwaukee, in Wayne. My family raised milking cows. We sell milk to cheese makers. It was a pretty good living. We weren't rich, but we did okay."

"How'd you survive the depression?"

"We didn't do too bad, the government needed beef and milk. We had over two-thousand head."

"Wow, does your parents still own the farm?" Jay noticed the pale look on his face. "My parents died in 1934."

"Sorry, I didn't know. Can I ask what happened?"

"They were delivering a tanker full of milk to a cheese factory near Madison. On the way home, a witness said that my father swerved when a dear ran across the road. The truck went in a ditch and flipped over a couple of times."

"Once again, I am sorry. Do you still own the farm?"

"I do, my uncle and younger brother are working it. At least my parents died together."

"Where were you when this happened?"

"I was an instructor with the US Army Field Artillery School in Fort Sill, Oklahoma. I trained the Army and Marines."

"I guess that your experience in France helped with your instructing." Jay replied. "It didn't hurt. I was training 19 to 24-year-old- kids. Some caught on very fast, others I wouldn't trust with a slingshot, if you know what I mean."

"I know exactly what you mean. These kids today would probably turn and run if they heard any gunfire." Jay added. "Well, I think I should go and find Alice to see what kind of trouble she's gotten herself in. Later Major."

Jay made his way back to the Pullman. When Jay got back, he couldn't find Alice. Alice was in her room napping. He decided to let her sleep for a while. Jay sat at the dining room table, going over what clues he may have. The funny thing is, he didn't have any clues. He hoped that Mike might have found out something.

After about twenty-minutes Alice appears from her room, rubbing her eyes. "It's about time you woke up." Jay said. Well, did you find out anything?" Alice asked. "I was at the bar talking to the Major. He told me that he owns a farm in Wisconsin and that in 1934 his parents died. I feel for the guy. First his parents died. Then two years later. If the Major didn't have bad luck, he wouldn't have any luck at all."

"I found out some juicy stuff. I was talking to Donatella. She told me that Giovanni was a womanizer. He had two affairs as far as she knows. He slept with Enzo's wife, that lasted almost a year." Jay listened intensely. "It didn't matter that Giovanni was his cousin. It seems like your friend had no morals. The second affair."

"Don't tell me, Mario."

"You got it Boss."

"I guess now that Mario is back on my list as my number one suspect and number two on the hit parade, Enzo. After scratching them off the list. I guess we have to look at this in a whole new light."

"So, what are we going to do now, tie them up with a hot light beaming down on them."

"Very funny, you watch to many Bogart and Cagney movies."

"The only movie I watch is the ADVENTURES of JAY JAX, which I co-star in."

"Okay I guess we'll just go back to what we've been doing. You watch Enzo and I'll stick with Mario. Let's see, we still have El Paso, Pensacola, Jacksonville, D.C. Then our last stop New York. We only have five more stops before we reach New York. When we stop at Fort Bliss, I'll call Mike to see if he found out anything. We're just going to have to have our eyes and ears opened. This assassin is going to make a mistake sooner or later."

"I never knew that Giovanni was such a lady killer. Goes to show you, you don't always know the person. Giovanni always seemed shy and recluse. I can't believe that his own cousins would kill him. I've been wrong before, I guess I'm wrong now. The thing that I can't figure is why all the killings. Any suggestions?"

"Maybe we're looking at this the wrong way. What if it's two separate cases." Alice explained her thoughts. "Maybe it was a robbery. The reason nothing was taken was because you were knocking at the door."

"That sounds good, there's only one thing wrong with that theory. Whoever it was had to take some time planning to make it look like a suicide. What ever happened we have to find out before they board the Manhattan. If not, we'll never know what the real story is, plus we still don't have a motive. I'm still leaning towards Mario and Enzo. Infidelity would be a huge motive. If either one of them is the killer. I'm afraid that some one's wife will be swimming to Berlin.

At that time Isaac came in with their lunch. It was a simple lunch, just sandwiches and beer. It seems like Jay and Alice does some serious drinking. When Alice drinks, she nurses the drink. As for Jay he didn't start drinking or smoking, he started these vices after his wife was murdered. He usually drinks to forget the past, except the only thing it does, is make it more depressing.

After lunch they just sat at the table trying to figure out what the hell was going on. Giovanni may have been a womanizer; they just don't know why he was murdered. Mario is now their number one suspect. Well, if that was the reason, we don't think killing Gio over a woman, I don't think so, but I've been wrong before, maybe I'm wrong now. Maybe Mario was capable of killing Giovanni. What are we missing.?" Jay asked Alice. "If Mario did kill him, he would be killing two birds with one stone. Mario would get rid of his competition, where is wife is concerned, then he becomes the lead. More prestige and more money."

"I don't think it would be about the affair; it would be more about him taking over in the opera." Jay explained. "So, Mario and Enzo are number one and number two on our suspect list."

It's now 0230. The cars are quiet with everyone sleeping. In the car in front of the Pullman you can see Dorothia, Wainsford's maid.

in the passageway. She's standing at the front of the car, at 0235 you can see a dark figure comes up to her. Haben Sie etwas fur mich, Frau Frohnhoefer?" The figure asked.

"Yes, I do, but I prefer English instead of German, I don't want to slip up. I have plans of the whole railroad system. I have the plans of the horseshoe curve near Altoona Pennsylvania. If we could destroy that section of track, the U.S. Will never recover.

"Frau, you did good, the Fuhrer will be please. Now go back to your room.

We won't see each other until we board the Manhattan.

# Chapter Twelve

The next day, they were still in the arid desert country of New Mexico, and the train windows had to be left open, but when they tried to open the windows, they wouldn't budge. Jay wasn't able to get it opened either, so they asked Isaac if he can get the window opened. Nothing it seems like the windows were painted shut. He said, "let me go fetch Miss Dottie. She knows the maintenance crew. We'll get them to come on board at the next stop."

Five minutes later Isaac returned with Dottie. She said, I'll have a maintenance foreman come and fix it."

"Thank you, Dottie," replied Jay. "Dottie, would you join us for dinner tonight? We haven't talked or even seen much of you this whole trip."

She answered, "I would love to."

"I'll have the Major join us. Then we could have a good dinner conversation. So, we'll see you at 1900."

"1900, I don't understand."

"I'm sorry, I always think that everyone knows military time. 1900 is 7:00," Jay explained. Jay then went looking for Major Hart. He wasn't in his room, or the bar. He finally found him in the observation car. "Major, would you like to join us for dinner?" Jay asked. "I would love to." The Major replied.

"Good, be there at 1900." At 1900 sharp Major Hart and Dottie came in together.

"Glad You's made it. Anyone care for a drink?" The Major ordered a bourbon, Dottie had schnapps, Jay had a beer and Alice had a dry martini. She said that Isaac makes the best martinis. They all sat at the dining room table. Isaac waited on them, while Chuma was cooking the finest prime rib, with all the trimmings.

"Now that we're all hear who wants to start. Tell us a little bit about yourselves, ask questions, nothing is off limits. The only one we can't talk about is Giovanni. Rest in peace." Alice started, "I went to the San Francisco University. For three years, I graduated in 1929. I worked in a bank for a while, then I read a want add. Some big shot private investigator was looking for a secretary. I did take Criminal Justice as my major. So, here I am still looking for this big shot P.I." Everyone looked at Jay and started to laugh.

Jay said, "Very, very funny. I'll start now. I grew up in New Jersey, my old man was a drunk. I adored my Little sister, who isn't that little anymore. I was in love with my childhood sweetheart, Angela. After I got back from France, I became a cop. My wife's father owned a bank, Angela worked as a teller. One day when I was out of town the bank was held up. My wife and a security guard were killed. Then I came to San Francisco and became a homicide detective. I was wounded spent almost a year in the hospital. Now I'm here.

Dottie was next to speak. "After the war I was working in housekeeping. When Mr. Wainsford was in Germany to sell railroad equipment, he saw me working, so he asked if I wanted to come to America and work for him. I told him that I would. The problem was the German government wouldn't give me permission to leave. It took almost three months before I got the okay."

Now it was the Major's turn. "Sorry about your wife. I joined the Army in 1917. I was in France in 1918. After the war I went home for a bit. Then I went back to the Army. Now I'm escorting an opera company around the world. So, that's my story.

After diner, all four of them started to play cards. The card game lasted for about two hours. Dottie was the big winner. Fifty dollars from Jay, thirty-five dollars from Alice and fifty-five from the Major.

Jay said, "I don't know about you guys, but I think Dottie is a professional card player."

After the card game they all had one drink for the road. "Dottie, Major thanks for coming. I had a good time. Alice?"

"I had a good time, too." The Major and Dottie left the Pullman at 2310. Jay and Alice decided to stay up for a while and have a few drinks. They wound up going to sleep around midnight.

# Chapter Thirteen

After breakfast they were just watching to scenery. The train pulled into the El Paso station. Buses were there to take them to the Plaza Hotel. There wasn't a show tonight. The show is at 1900 at Fort Bliss Army Base tomorrow. That gave everyone a break.

When Jay and Alice got to their rooms, Jay put a call in to Mike.

"Sgt. Murphy, it's Jay, is Mike in?" Murphy said, "He's in, but right now he's in a meeting. It should be rapping up soon. Hold on." Jay waited on the phone for only three minutes. Then he heard Mike answer his phone. "Homicide Lt. Morris."

"Mike it's Jay, did you find anything out?"

"I talked to Sgt. Woodman at the Presidio; he told me that they're trying to get German spies. It seems like this country has a spy problem. He told me that the Fed's got an eye on someone from El Paso. He's a professor at the University of Texas. His name is Walter Dietrich."

Jay told Mike, "that's a German name if I ever heard one. You would figure if you're a spy, you'll be able to come up with a better alias. He probably used his real name. I thought these spies were smart."

"He even teaches German and chemistry. If you can, see if you can make contact with Mr. Dietrich. Look him up and down, see if you can get a read on him." Mike told him.

Jay replied, "I know just how we could approach him. I'll call the University after I hang up with you. Me and Alice will go there and act like parents of a daughter that just graduated from high school. And she was thinking about chemistry, and she heard that the University of Texas has an excellent chemistry program. That way the admissions department would take us to see Mr. Dietrich. I'll let you know if I find out anything." After he hung up the phone, he called Alice to his room. "Tomorrow around noon time. Mr. Jay and Mrs. Alice Jax are go Into college."

"What's the deal?"

"We are going to the University of Texas to enroll our daughter in their chemistry classes. Mike wants us to meet Professor Walter Dietrich." He told her.

Alice said, "I didn't know we had a daughter. I guess you had to be there."

After Jay explained to Alice what he was planning He called the University of Texas. "Hello, University of Texas, how may I help you?"

"Me and my wife are vacationing on our way to New Orleans. Our daughter graduates' high school this month and she heard that you have an excellent chemistry program."

"Yes, we have an excellent chemistry program."

"Great, can we come by tomorrow, say around noon. Would it be possible to speak to the chemistry professor?"

"I'm sure that can be arranged. One thing Professor Dietrich loves, is women who want to be chemist, usually reserved for men."

"Okay, we'll be there tomorrow at noon. It's been a pleasure talking to you."

"When you come ask anyone where the Admissions Office is. They know that you are coming to enroll your daughter, um."

"Oh, I'm sorry, her name is Victoria."

"Okay your daughter Victoria wants to enroll. I'll make sure that Professor Dietrich will be here. Goodbye."

"Goodbye," Jay hung up.

"Well Mrs. Jax we have an appointment tomorrow at the college, so, we can register Victoria." They both stared to laugh.

That night they went to dinner with Major Hart. "So, Major what do you have on your schedule tonight and tomorrow before curtain time," Jay asked. "Tonight, I don't have anything planned. I'm just going to stay in my room tonight and reflect on what's happened.

Tomorrow I'll most likely walk around downtown, maybe I'll by the wife something."

"Wife, you never told me that you were married, keeping secrets, are we."

The Major added, "I think that I'll go on my nightly constitutional. See you in the morning for breakfast?"

"Okay, later. Have a nice walk." It was close to 2100. So, Alice and Jay decided to go, you guessed it, the bar to have a few drinks, before retiring they took the elevator to the roof where there was a roof top bar.

# Chapter Fourteen

2200, Professor Dietrich is in Pioneer Park. Sitting on a bench near the lake. 2215 he sees someone approach him. Park lights were dime, but it lit the walkway behind the silhouette. The figure walks up to Dietrich and sits alongside of him.

"Do you have anything for me, Lieutenant?" the figure asked him. "Yes, I do. I've been giving some of the American soldiers' German lessons."

"Do you think that was wise?"

"I do. I have many locations were their Sherman tanks are stored. Number of troops and where they go on training maneuvers."

"You did well lieutenant. The Fuhrer will be pleased, I wouldn't be surprised if you get a medal."

"Vielen Dank."

"You're very welcomed lieutenant. You can go home now. Dietrich rose to leave. He turned right to start walking back to the University. Just then the figure put his left hand around his head. Holding his hand over Dietrich's mouth, so he couldn't scream out. With the right hand he took a knife and trust it in the back of his neck, with an upward angle. Then he threw Dietrich's body in the lake, followed by the knife.

In the morning Jay and Alice joined the Major for breakfast. "The Major spoke first, "so what's on your schedule today?"

"I have an old friend at Fort Bliss, I haven't seen him since 1924. So, I figure that I would surprise him."

"Are you sure that he's still there?" The Major asked. "He better be, he's the Sargent Major of the base."

Jay really did have a friend at Fort Bliss. He couldn't tell anyone that they were going to the University. Everyone still thinks that they were on vacation.

At 1130 Jay and Alice caught a cab to the University. They arrived at 1150. Jay paid the cab driver and started to the Main Building. They went inside and asked the first person that they saw where the admission office was. The student pointed the way. Jay knocked on the door. He heard someone tell them to come in. When they walked into the office the woman behind the desk was obviously crying.

Jay wanted to ask what was wrong, but he thought better of it. "You's must be Mr. & Mrs. Jax. You want to enroll your daughter in classes here." Then Jay said, "we also would like to meet Professor Dietrich." When Jay said that the secretary burst out in tears. Jay asked, "what's wrong?"

"Professor Dietrich was killed last night. Everybody is taking it hard, everyone loved him."

"Can I ask what happened."

"Last night the Professor went to Pioneer Park. I really don't know what happened. All's I know his body was found by the police in Pioneer Lake. They're not saying much."

"I am so sorry Miss. Maybe we should go. We'll be back in August."

"That's fine. Maybe the shock of what happened will be in the past."

They started to leave the Admission Office, Jay turned around and said, "I am truly sorry." Alice said, "that's strange, the night before we were to meet him, he dies. Something is definitely going on. I wonder if it was a heart, or something else."

"I don't know why dead people keep following us. We know that the killer is on the train. The killer did try to kill me in the baggage car. With Mussolini on the war path. Hitler and Mussolini are friends. I'm starting to mistrust the Italians. Maybe Mussolini gave the order to kill him. He probably knew that Giovanni had many friends in the states. Our two main suspects are still Mario and Enzo. My bet is on

Mario. I just realized something; we haven't seen Mario for a while. I just can't go up to him and ask for an alibi for last night." Alice said, "I guess we just have to go back to the old routine. You follow Mario and I'll stick to Enzo."

When they got back to the hotel, Mario was just getting into a cab. Jay had no time to react. The cab was gone before Jay paid the cabby.

Jay and Alice went back to the roof top bar. Jay had a beer and high classed Alice had another martini. Jay said to Alice, "I don't know how you can drink that shit. Martinis taste like rubbing alcohol."

Alice snapped back with a sly grin, "I like rubbing alcohol. Just don't light a match in near me."

They went to dinner at 1600. They joined Major Hart, at the table were Donatella and Rosie Gallo. Jay didn't want to bring up Giovanni's death. Everyone still thought that they were on vacation, everyone except the killer. Jay was looking around, something wasn't right. Then he realized. "Major, where's Mario?" The Major replied, "he's not performing tonight. This afternoon he went to town to have lunch at an Italian restaurant. When he got back to the hotel, he was in such pain he decide that he would stay in and nurse his stomach. I don't know if it was food poisoning, or that it's been a while since he had an Italian dinner. Enzo's his understudy, so he will take the lead."

There was no way Jay could make up an excuse why he had to stay behind. That did make him more suspicious of Mario, but there wasn't anything that he could do.

After dinner they all went out to get on the buses. Fort Bliss was seven miles from the hotel. The bus ride would seem to take longer. The temperature outside was ninety-degrees, at least the hotel had air conditioning. Luckily, the opera was going to be in the base theater, like the hotel the theater was air conditioned. It took twenty-minutes to get to the base.

Dorothia, "Dottie" even came with us. Usually, she either stays on the train, or she stays at the hotel. It was starting to get a little cooler out. The temperature was down to eighty degrees now.

The show started promptly at 1900. It was comfortable inside the theater. At intermission Jay went out and had a smoke. It was much cooler now. Must have been in the sixties.

Jay asked Alice, "so, did you see anything out of the ordinary?"

"No, haven't seen anything Boss. Enzo never left the theater. Nothing unusual."

"Same here. Everything was quiet, except for the opera. I swear by the time we get to New York I'll know this damn opera by heart. The only thing I'm not happy about, is that Mario stayed at the hotel. That really puts everything in focus. Mario could be up to anything. I wish I could have stayed at the hotel. I would be able to tell if he really was sick or was just a rouse."

Alice said, "well we're just going to focus on him. Are we forgetting about Enzo?

"No, he's still number two on the suspect list. Who knows, maybe their working together.

Jay and Alice were getting frustrated. They knew that they were getting close. Why else would someone take a shot at him. They couldn't put two and two together.

The opera ended at 2200. The General in charge of the base invited everyone to the Officer's Mess. The General told Major Hart that it was going to be an after party. "There will be plenty to eats, and drinks. It's the Army's way of saying thank you."

The after party ended at 2330. It was cool out, so the trip back to El Paso shouldn't be that bad. The buses got back to the hotel at 0025. (12:25am) Everyone were pretty exhausted. As usual Jay and Alice went up to the Rooftop Bar, for a night cap. The bar was closing at 0100. They had one drink at the bar, then took a drink back to their rooms.

They both went into their rooms, but as soon as Alice entered her room she went right over to the adjoining doors and opened it.

"Jay, want to finish the drink on my balcony, while we discuss what we're doing."

Jay replied, "sounds good, I have to get out of this suit first. Also, I want to give Mike a call."

"Okay, see you in a little bit," said Alice.

Jay changed then went to the phone to call Mike.

"San Francisco Police Department Sargent Murphy. How can I help you?"

"Pat, Jay here is Mike in? I need to talk to him."

"Boy Jay you do have good timing. Mike is standing right in front of me. Mike said that he'll take the call in his office. Officer Murphy called Mike's extension. The phone only rang four times, then Mike answered. "Jay, what's the word? Did you get a chance to talk to Professor Dietrich?" Well, me and Alice went to the University to enroll our daughter Victoria in their science program."

"And" Mike asked.

"Strange thing. He died last night in a park. I haven't a clue on how he died. Maybe you could call the El Paso Police to find out exactly what happened. They'll most likely tell a cop, instead of a couple of tourists."

"Will do Jay, first thing in the morning. I'll also talk to my friend at The Presidio to see if he knows anything. Call me when you get to Pensacola, maybe I'll know something by then."

After he spoke to Mike, he made his way to Alice's room, he knocked twice the walked in, Alice was on the balcony taking in the cool breeze.

"Alice, you look comfortable. Did you get any ideas?"

"Nothing yet boss, as a matter of fact I wasn't even thinking about the case. I'm just thinking how beautiful the city is at night, you can hear an occasional car horn in the distance. That's about it, and you?"

"Mike told me that he's going to call the El Paso Police in a couple of days and try to find out how Dietrich died. I'll give you ten to one they found a knife wound in the back of his skull. That seems to be the S.O.P. on these killings. We're leaving tomorrow at 0800. It's about a two-day trip to Pensacola. I would still like to get into the baggage car again and go through some luggage."

"Do you think that's wise? Remember what happened last time, I almost wound up minus a partner. Whoever it is they can see you going back there. So, most likely it will happen again. Why don't we try this? It's had to come up with an excuse why we're not going to the show. We have to wait until the luggage, performers, crew are at the same place at the same time, like when the show is going on. The luggage would be in the staging area at the Carnegie Hall. Hopefully we'll be able to search uninterrupted. Well, that's only me thinking out loud."

"Alice your supposed to be working for me, not the other way around. How do you come up with this stuff? My thought was to search as soon as we can. I like that thought of yours. We're still going to find out the whole story before we get to New York. New York would be cutting it close, but I think we can do it. Well, I guess we can call it a night. Breakfast at 0630?"

"A girl has to get her beauty sleep. Night Jay, see you in the morning."

Jay headed back to his room, took a shower, then turned in. "Goodnight Angela." Jay says goodnight to Angela mostly every night, or at least tried to. Jay had a rough night trying to sleep. In his dream he was back in France. His dreams about France always started with him and his spotter in no man's land. He's looking through his scope on his sniper rifle. He sees, what he thinks he sees. Is a German about to execute another German. Jay was thinking maybe the one who is about to be executed was a deserter. Jay's job was to kill German's. He aimed at the German standing. His spotter tells him that he doesn't see any German's. Jay squeezes the trigger. He hears the crack of the round leaving the barrel. Everything was going in slow motion. You can actually see the bullet flying through the air. It felt like it took one whole day to reach his target. He sees the round go through the German's neck, almost knocking his head clean off. After the round makes its mark the one to be executed fell on the ground. Jay thought maybe he took too long to fire, and the German carried out the execution.

He tells his spotter to watch his back while he crawls to were the body was. He was about 300 yards away. It took almost two- and one-half hours to make it to the scene.

He checks the German he shot. The German was on his stomach, the weird thing he was on his stomach, while his head was on his back staring at Jay. Jay went over to the corpse, reached down, and moved the head so it's face is on the ground.

He walks over to see if the man was still alive. He notices that the man isn't wearing a German uniform, not even English. Jay could see that the man was trying to play dead and doing a poor job of it.

Jay took his rifle, put it under the man's left shoulder. Turned him over. "You might as well open your eyes soldier, you're not dead, yet." As soon as the man opens his eyes Jay wakes up.

He looks at his clock. 5:37am. He figured that he might as well get up. He goes and takes a shower. Lied down on his bed when he finished his shower. At 5:55 he decided to get dressed before Alice comes in. He was lying on his bed naked. Alice has a habit of knocking once and comes in.

It only took Jay around four minutes to get his shirt, pants, and socks, when there's a knock on his door. This time she knocked twice. She asked, "are you decent?" then walked right in.

Jay said, "I'm just putting on my shoes."

"Well hurry up, I'm starving," she said.

# Chapter Fifteen

Alice asked him, "are you okay? You look a little flushed."

Jay said, "I'm fine, I just had another dream last night. It was about the time I met Giovanni, after saving is life. The funny thing about saving his life is, that a little later Giovanni saved my life. When that Kraut tried to shoot me in the back of my head."

Something seemed a little off to him this morning. He just couldn't put his finger on it. He sat there for about ten-minutes. "Well, this isn't getting me anywhere. Snap out of it," he said to himself, something he hasn't done in a while. After he said goodnight to Angela something started to seem a little off. He just thought that it was fatigue. He got dressed, then walked over to Alice's door, just then Alice knocked on his door, scaring him half to death. Alice opened the door and walked into his room.

"Ready for a hearty breakfast for our last time in El Paso? Oh, I forgot, we have to come back in August to enroll Victoria in the University," she said with a giggle.

"Very funny, your sister is the dramatic actress, you should have been a comedic actress," Jay said back.

They went toward the elevator. Donatella was waiting at the elevator, with Rosey.

"Morning ladies. Ready to get back on the train?"

"We are, but we will be happy when this damn tour is over and we're back in Italy," Donatella said.

"Maybe Italy isn't a place one should be at this time," Jay said. "Mussolini seems to be on the warpath. I just figured that it would be safer anywhere else," Jay added.

Rosie spoke first, "I'm not crazy about the man, but he is our leader. I have a friend that is Mussolini's niece. We were talking just before we went on tour, she said that he's doing good things for the Italian people. We have a low unemployment rate. It seems that he's putting everyone to work. I think Italy is going to be just fine."

"I hope you're right Rosie, I've grown close to all of you. I'd hate to see something happen to you guys," Jay told them. "Is everyone packed? We board the train in less than an hour," Jay asked.

When they got to the restaurant it was jumping. Major Hart was holding a table for them. This time Mario and Enzo were at the table.

"Great," Jay thought to himself. Alice just had a weird look on her face. Alice sat next to Rosie, Alice was on Jay's right and Donatella on his left. It was Enzo on his left and Donatella on his right. On Donatella left were the two young stagehands, Marco and Carmine. The last three chairs were Enzo, Dottie and Major Hart.

Jay started the conversation, "so, tours almost over. Major, how many more stops are there?

"Well after here we have Pensacola, then Jacksonville, D.C. then New York. Then we board the Manhattan for Berlin. To tell you the truth, I really don't want to go to Berlin. We've been invited to the Olympics. So, the brass says go, I go. I'm sure you know what I mean."

"That's right, the brass says jump you ask how high," Jay replied. "I think that I would go if I had the chance. Haven't been to Germany since 1919. Well, let me correct myself, I have never been in Germany. I spent all my time in France. Maybe it would be better is I just stay put. I wind up visiting France every night. I never use to have nightmares about the war, but after my wife died the nightmares started," Jay added.

"I'm pretty fortunate I never have bad dreams," said the Major. "How about you Alice, ever want to take a trip to Europe?" The Major asked.

"I always wanted to go to Paris. I think I'll wait 'till things cool down," Alice replied. Alice then spoke to Carmine and Marco, "so boys what did you like the United States?"

The two boys didn't know a lick of English. So, Dottie translated.

Dottie started to translate. "The boys said that they love America and wished that they could stay. Marco said that he wasn't that crazy about bretos, to spice."

"You mean burritos, a Mexican dish. Some can be quite spicy. The Mexican food is great, after you get use to them," Jay explained.

Jay started to read the morning newspaper. There was an article on the front page of the El Paso Tribune. He excused himself and took Alice out into the lobby. "Alice, do you still have Dietrich's address," Jay asked her. "I still have it. Why?"

"Let me see it." Alice reaches into her purse and hands Jay her notebook. Jay looked at the address, then back to the paper.

"I just read a news article about an apartment fire last night. It was Dietrich's apartment. Several people died and eight are in critical condition. I doubt that it was an accident."

Alice asked, "are you going to tell the cops in what we know?"

"No if I did, we'll be here for days. We have to find this bastard soon. Before more die."

"How are we going to do that, when we have no idea who it is?"

"I'm hoping that he would make a mistake. What mistake, I don't know." Jay through the paper in the garbage and returned to the dining room. They were only gone for about five minutes. After they sat down to continue with their breakfast the Major asked if everything was all right.

Jay said, "everything is good. I dropped my wallet somewhere. I was going to send Alice back to my room, to see if I left it there, but when I went to the front desk, they had it."

They finished breakfast and made their way to the buses. The station was only four blocks from the hotel, so they were there in a matter of minutes. They left most of their luggage on the train, Jay and Alice only had one bag a piece. As soon as they put their luggage on the train, they disappeared. Isaac was fast. Jay never saw him take the bags into the Pullman. They settled down for their two-day trip to Pensacola.

# Chapter Sixteen

It was hot in the Louisiana bayou, but the maintenance men had been able to get Jay's stateroom window opened. There was now a decent breeze cooling them. They both sipped cold beer and watched the swampland go by.

"You know, there was something I forgot to tell that Mike had told me. She put on her listening face.

"This tour is more high level and diplomatic than we ever thought. It seems that the Defense Department agreed to Mussolini's suggestion to have the Italian opera company do a tour of military bases. Mussolini is close to Hitler these days. It's a tour of military bases, and it will extend to the 1936 Olympics in Berlin. Our State Department, for some reason, thought it was a good idea."

"So," she said, "were probably not too far off that the theme is correct."

"That's my thinking. Do you know where we're staying in Pensacola,"

Jay asked.

"I believe that it's the Pensacola Grand Hotel. Someone told me that it's a beautiful place. Big and gaudy."

Forty-one hours later they pulled into the Pensacola train station. When they left the train, they were a bit taken back. Inside the station there was a small Navy band, as soon as the opera troupe entered the station the band started to play the Italian National Anthem. Jay said, "I have an idea. If you're not game, just tell me. I'm serious. Don't feel obligated."

Alice smiled, "wow, sounds serious."

"Yesterday we said that we can't follow everyone in the troupe."

"Yeah?"

"But we can follow two of them."

"And they are, of course, Enzo and Mario?"

"I knew I picked well when I hired you.

"Who do I get?"

"I get Mario. Enzo is yours. We might lose them in the crowd after the show, so I was thinking that we find some pretense to go backstage, then we can find our man."

"Sounds exciting. Never thought I would become a real P.I."

"You're going to find out that there's nothing exciting about tailing someone. It's worrisome. First, you have to stay far enough behind him so that you're not obviously following them. That's when you have to get creative, like you're window-shopping, tying your shoe. Stuff like that. Well, for you, it would be putting on lipstick or something. Bottom line is that you have to be sure that they don't make you. Once they know you're suspicious of them, everything gets harder."

"Yeah, especially when both Enzo and Mario knows us."

"Exactly. Do you think you can do that?"

She didn't answer immediately. When she did, she said, "I think I can look innocent enough. These guys don't know you're a P.I., do they?"

"I don't see how, unless someone checked me out. And if they did check, that only points the finger in their direction. Of course, you realize we are only speculating."

"Okay Boss, let's do it."

After the show ended, they all boarded the buses. Jay, Alice and Major Hart took a cab back to the hotel.

It took Jay's cab about ten-minutes to get back to the hotel. Jay and Alice sat on a bench in front of the hotel. The Major went right to the bar. The buses arrived twenty-minutes later. It was now 2054. "10:54pm".

The buses started to empty out. As soon as Mario and Enzo got off the bus, they both hoped into a cab. Jay and Alice got up quickly and grabbed their own cab. Jay told the cabby to follow them. It seemed like they we're heading downtown.

When Mario's cab got to town, they stopped at an Italian restaurant. Jay didn't want to follow them right into the restaurant, so they made the cabby drive around the block so they would be on the opposite side of the street where Alice noticed a café right across the street. They stopped in front of the café. They went into the café and sat at a table by a window. That way they can have some drinks while they watch the restaurant. Jay ordered a beer and Alice just had a cup of tea and a pastry.

"I wish I knew what was going on in there. I know that they're eating. I just wish I knew what they were talking about," Jay said.

Alice said, "who knows maybe they're talking about the weather, or talking about home. Well, let's just wait and see where they go from here."

"I guess you're right. Maybe they had nothing to do with this. We could be barking up the wrong tree. Except they're the only two that had something to gain. Don't forget, something similar took place many years ago, involving two brothers. On killed the other when he was being ignored. That's when Cane killed Able just because he thought God was ignoring him," Jay said.

Alice asked, "what, are you getting biblical on me? I never figured you being religious or anything."

Jay told her, "I use to go to church every Sunday. Me and Angela were regular church goers. She was brought up Catholic. I was Catholic myself. I went to church with my mother and my little sister Gail. My old man was always too drunk to go to church. When Angela was shot, I stayed at her bedside for two days, I prayed to God for hours not to take her. She died the second day. After that I didn't have much for religion anymore. I may have stopped going to church, but I still know my bible.

They waited for about an hour when they saw Mario and Enzo leave the restaurant. The area was a popular restaurant location, so there were plenty of cabs in the area. It was now close to 0100. Mario and Enzo caught a cab and left. Luckily there was cab right in front of the café. When they got into the cab Jay used that familiar fraise you her in a gangster movie. "FOLLOW THAT CAB."

Jay thought that this cab driver has done this before. He staid far enough behind their cab but made sure that he wouldn't lose them. They followed the cab through town. It looked like they were just going back to the hotel. Mario and Enzo's cab made a right-hand turn, they were back at the hotel. Jay instructed the driver to drop the off at the side of the hotel, he didn't want to show up right behind them. Jay paid the cab driver, then walked down the street. When they got to the hotel entrance Mario and Enzo were still in front of the hotel. It was now 0115.

When they got by the two Italians, Jay greeted them, "morning gentleman. Out late I see. You two weren't up to no good, were you?"

Enzo answered, "no Signor, we just went into town to get some real Italian food. You two been out for walk?"

"Yea, Enzo, neither of us could sleep. So, we went for a walk, we figured that the walk would make us sleepy?"

Then Alice spoke up, "the walk not only made me tired, made my feet sore. Now my feet are killing me. Jay no more midnight walks for me!"

The four of them walked to the elevators. When they got to their floor, they said goodnight and disappeared into their room. Jay and Alice walked over to their rooms, said goodnight then disappeared into their rooms.

They had to get to sleep, because tomorrow the buses are leaving the hotel at 0900. They were leaving a little late. That way everyone could take their time at breakfast.

# Chapter Seventeen

Jay woke up at 0645. Took a shower and got dressed. He went over to the adjoining rooms door. Knocked twice then entered Alice's room.

"Alice, you decent?"

"Be out in five."

While Jay waited for Alice he sat at her desk and read the morning newspaper. An article caught his eye.

"Last night at 9:00 pm at the Naval Air Station there was an accident. It seems that a warehouse worker drove his car of off the PENSACOLA BAY BRIDGE. The driver Otto Zimmerman drowned."

When Alice came out of the bathroom Jay showed her the article. Alice said, "that can't be? Can it? At that time, we were at the opera. I guess someone could have snuck away. Like you said, we can't watch everyone."

"I know, it's just a coincidence that it happened during the show. Be sides his name was Otto Zimmerman Well we can't worry about that now."

The buses arrived at 0830. As usual Jay, Alice and the Major took a cab to the station. It will take the train about seven hours to Jacksonville. The train was located on a siding. They got to the station about twenty-minutes before the buses arrived.

The three entered the train as soon as they got to the station. They went into the Pullman Car and sat at the dining room table. A few minutes later the major got up from his chair and said, "can you please excuse me. I think that I'll do some snooping around before the buses showed up." Jay responded, "good idea Major. That way you'll have some privacy."

"Be back in a bit."

While the Major did his snooping Jay and Alice where just going to relax. "So, Jay where do we stand with theories?" Alice asked.

"Haven't a clue, maybe the Major will come up with something. We only have two more stops before we make New York. Maybe this boils down to an assassination plot to kill Roosevelt. That sounds farfetched, but we can't put any possibility aside."

Alice answered, "I hope you're wrong. We are sitting with the President, aren't we?"

"I'm pretty sure we will be close. Wainsford and Roosevelt are friends, and I believe he contact the White House. Wainsford doesn't buy this vacation we're on. He's sure that we're investigating on our own. I doubt he mentioned what's going on."

The buses arrived and everyone boarded. Five minutes after the buses arrived the Major made his way back.

"Well Major, find anything interesting? Asked Jay.

"Nothing out of the ordinary. I did search a few bags that were left on the train, with no success. If whoever killed Giovanni, they're doing a bang-up job of avoiding suspicion. I can't figure out if the killing was a spere of the moment, or something planned well in advance. I'm stumped," said the Major.

"Welcome to the club. Can you think of any suspects? I'd say that maybe it's a German. Except the only German on board is Dottie. I doubt if she killed him. She was nowhere near the Opera House. The only other suspects would be the Italians. That would give you over twenty suspects. I'm glad that it's your problem. I'm sorry Major I didn't mean to have it come out like that," Jay apologies.

"I know you didn't mean it. This situation is just getting more confusing. I'm not an investigator, so I have no idea what I'm doing. I'm an artillery officer. What do I know about investigating a murder. NOTHING!!" Said the Major.

I don't know what to say Major, the only thing I know is Insurance and my agency. I could sell you some life insurance." Jay said.

Jay had to make up an occupation. He choose insurance, because one of his closest friends was an insurance salesman. "Major join us for lunch?"

"I'll be there," replied the Major.

After the Major left, they decided that they were going to relax. They weren't even going to discuss the case. The train ride was only a few hours away. Alice went to her room and got a little sleep. She told Jay, "wake me for lunch or if there's another murder. Especially if it's you."

"Very funny. Just go the sleep and I'll wake you for lunch, or if I get killed," Jay said with a sly grin on his face.

The train was haff way Jacksonville, they were just getting into Tallahassee. I It was now 1130, so Jay went into Alice's room to wake her. Jay entered her room, he stopped by her dressing table and just looked at her. She was lying on her back. Even though she was sleeping her hair looked perfect. She was gorgeous, he came back to reality. He didn't go up to her. He told her that it was never a good idea to wake up a Marine. He was just thinking what might happen if he wakes a "BEAUTY". So, he decided to call to her from the dressing table. It's been a long trip, but he has never been in her room while she was sleeping. In a soft voice, "Alice, it's 1130 time to get up."

He got no response, so he whispered to her again. He did called to her three more times, nothing. Then at the top of his lungs came this. "ALICE WAKE UP." Before she had a chance to kill him, he left the room as fast as he could.

About five minutes later she came out. "Are you insane? I almost had a heart attack," yelling at him.

"Have you forgotten about the window shade a few weeks ago," he asked. "Oh, I forgot about that. Well, I guess we're even." They both started laughing. Just then there's a knock on their door. Jay figured that it was the Major.

"Come on in Major."

As the Major entered the room he said, "Boy, you're trusting. What if I was the killer?"

"Well, I guess we would be up SHITS CREEK WITHOUT a PADDLE. Now that we know that you aren't the kill, are you ready for lunch?"

"You bet; I'm starving. What's on the menu?" the Major asked.

"I think it's beef stew. Chuma doesn't want use to be to full when we get to Jacksonville," Alice told him. Alice added, "Chuma is one of the best chef's I ever seen."

During lunch everyone just sat around telling stories, that most likely were lies. Nobody cared. This was the first time during this whole trip where everyone was very relaxed. Alice talked about when she was at the University of San Francisco, telling them some secrets about how her and a few friends use to always getting into trouble, at least that's what it seemed. Jay mostly talked about his wife Angela. The major told stories ho he and his younger brother almost burnt the barn down. Everyone was having a good old time.

The train just went through Live Oak, there was only about an hour to Jacksonville. Everyone left to go back to their rooms, or wherever. Alice and Jay just decided to relax. They started to dose. Now they only had less than an hour before they arrived in Jacksonville.

The train pulled into the station at 1430, when the group exited the train there was a police escort to take them to the hotel, the Chief of Police was even there. Jay, Alice, and the Major rode in the Chief's car. Jay thought to himself, "I never saw a Chief of Police drive himself. There were eight squad cars, seven police officers counting thew Chief. When they were all in their assigned transportation.

The hotel was about an hour away. It was 87 degrees and about 100 degrees in the buses. The Chief thought ahead and had plenty water on the buses. There was also a sea breeze and with all the windows open the heat wasn't too bad.

The buses arrived at the hotel at 1540. The rooms for the opera company were all paid in advanced, Mr. Wainsford paid all of the SLEUTHS rooms. Every room had a balcony facing the Atlantic Ocean. As usual the PI's had adjoining rooms. They settled in their rooms for a while before they went to dinner.

# Chapter Eighteen

Everyone met in the main dining room at 1800. Jay, Alice, Major Hart, and Dottie sat together. Everyone was quite quiet at first. Then Jay asked the Major, "so, Major how long are you staying in Berlin?

The Major answered, "we will be there for a few days. I heard that the opera company is supposed to have an audience with Hitler. I think that Berlin is going to be something."

Jay replied, "when you get back from Germany, give me a call. I'd love to hear what Hitler is like. I kind of wish that I could go with you, but I haven't been home for five years. It'll be nice to see my sister again."

Alice asked, "so, what's on the agenda for today? I was thinking that Jay and me go to town and do some shopping. My money is burning a hole in my pocket."

Mario spoke up, "me, I think that I may go swimming. Being we're so close to the ocean. As a matter of fact, I think the whole group is going swimming. Marco and Carmine told me that they can't wait to go swimming in the Atlantic Ocean. They never saw the Atlantic before. When those two get home, they'll be telling all of their friends about the adventure they've had, in the U.S.A. after diner it seemed that everyone went in opposite directions. Jay and Alice just went outside and sat in some lounge chairs, looking at the ocean and feeling the sea breeze caressing their bodies.

Alice asked, "well, what now?"

"I guess we relax for a while. I heard that the Major is going swimming too. Do you want to take a dip?" he asked Alice.

She replied, "no, what I wasn't to do is to go into town and spend some of those thousand dollars that's burning a hole in my pocket. Never had that much money before. I may even buy something for your sister."

The opera was scheduled for 1900 tomorrow. So, everyone could relax away from the train and theater.

Jay and Alice decided that after they check into their rooms. (They still checked into separate room). They didn't want anyone to know that they are a couple now. They always had rooms with adjoining rooms.

Jay, Alice, and the Major checked in. They decided to check the bar out. They got a booth in the corner. Jay spoke up first, "Major I bet you'll be clad when this trip is over."

"That's an understatement. I have to explain why Giovanni took his own life. He didn't seem upset or depressed. I wonder what happened between Hawaii and San Francisco. Did he contact you at all?" Asked the Major.

"A week ago, I received a letter from him. It had two tickets, other than that he didn't say anything else", replied Jay. Then he added, "well we're here on vacation. Me and Alice are doing tourist things today. We're not going to dwell on it. I'm sure that you'll be able to figure it out. Just let me know the verdict." Jay didn't want to mention his thoughts about Mario and Enzo.

"Where are use heading first," asked the Major.

"Don't really know yet. I have to look at a map. That way we can walk it. We'll try to go to the first one that's in line with all the other Monuments. We'll most likely walk to all the Monuments. Besides that, we been couped up so much on the train. Walking would give the both of us some exercise.

They only had one drink, then they got up and headed to the door to hail a cab. The cab dropped them off at the Lincoln Memorial. Jay could see that Alice was all excited. Never in her wildest dreams that she would wind up in Washington D.C., she looked like a little girl who just met Santa Claus. They visited all of the Monuments and Museums. After about three hours they made their way to the hotel. Mr. Wainsford called and paid for their rooms in advance. It's good to have friends in high places.

It was about 1400 by the time they got back to the hotel. They found Mario and Enzo in the lobby. They went over to the pair sitting at some chairs.

Jay asked them, "so, what are you guys up to?

Mario answered, "we decided to go to the Italian Embassy, we have a few friends working there. It's been a while since we've seen them.

"Well gentlemen have a good time reminiscing," Jay answered. Jay walked back to Alice. "So, what did they say," Alice asked. "They said that they were going to the Italian Embassy to see some old friends. I'm a little nervous with them going to the Embassy. Italy is under a Mussolini dictatorship and is Germany allies. My suspicions are looking more real now. We have to find out what's going on before they get on the ship, if they get on the ship, we'll never know what happened," Jay added.

Alice said, "I have faith in you, BOSS, if anyone can figure it out, you can." Jay said, "well kid I'm glad that you hold me in such high standers." They went back up to their rooms. They were going to forgo tonight's performance. They were going to relax the rest of the night. They didn't even go to the bar. They had room service bring up dinner and drinks. They were going to sleep in a little bit, their train wasn't leaving until around 0900. When they get to Philadelphia, they were going to change engines.

New York doesn't let trains in the city unless they're electric. There was going to be a two-hour layover in Philly.

# Chapter Nineteen

They weren't going exploring, instead. Alice said, "you know something I was always told that the Philly Cheese Steak was the best food to eat when in Philadelphia. So, that's what I want. Do we have to go anywhere special?

"No, they probably have a place right here in the station. Let's take a walk."

They headed down the concourse to see if they can find a "PHILADEPHIA CHEESESTEAK" place. They didn't have to walk to far. Alice's eyes popped when she saw people eating these cheesesteaks. Jay walked up to the counter and ordered two cheesesteaks and two beers. Jay looked around and didn't see anyone from the train. Jay was wondering why they were staying on the train.

Jay said to Alice, "did you see anyone from the train? I don't think anybody got off. Which is kind of odd. Finish your sandwich and let's get back on the train."

Alice gulped down her sandwich. They went back to the train. While they made their way to the train, Jay looked to the right. He saw Mario was on the phone.

Jay asked, "I wonder who he's calling?" Jay walked over to Mario; he was hoping that he would be able to hear some of the conversation. Just as he got close to the phone Mario hung up. He didn't want to ask Mario to whom he was talking. He didn't want to seem nosey. At that time there was an announcement over the P.A. system. Their train was starting to board. As they got to the train, they saw Dorothia. She got back on the train like she never left it. She looked at us and gave us a smile like the cat ate the canary. Just then Major Hart slapped his hand on the back of Jay's shoulder. "Ready to finish the journey? I myself will be glad once we're on the Manhattan. This whole trip has been a disaster for me. I'm wondering how much trouble I'm in," said the Major.

Jay said to him, "I wouldn't worry too much about it. One thing that I found out it the Marine Corps is that they know that shit happens."

"I hope you're right, I'd hate to lose my commission, or worst if you know what I mean?

"Major, would you like to join us for a fond well drink? I know that there's going to be a little bon voyage party. I don't know if Alice and me going, this trip has taken its toll on both of us. I'm just going to get tickets for the rest of our trip home. Maybe when you get home, we can get to have dinner some night," said Jay.

"Sounds good, I should be back in the states in about four weeks," the Major replied.

Jay replied, "that would be perfect, my wife's uncle owns the best Italian restaurant on the east coast. Here's the phone number and address of the hotel we'll be staying at. You'll love this hotel, it's at Boynton Beach, it a small resort area. Many movie stars go there for vacations."

They had a parting drink, then the Major went back to his room. They were only about two and a half hours from the city. Jay and Alice realized that time was running out. With the opera and the after party they only had around four hours to figure things out. They were going to distance themselves' s from the opera company. That way they would be able to snoop around without any interference. As the train past Edison, New Jersey Jay looked out on the train overlooking the farms as they passed by. Edison was only about twenty miles away from home. The train made a quick stop in Newark to pick up some bigshots and dignitaries. In less than forty-five minutes they'll be pulling into New York. The first two days the opera company had some free time to explore the big city.

As the train settled at the platform everyone started to collect their luggage. Jay and Alice had all their luggage with them.

Isaac entered their car and asked, "want me to help you with your luggage? It's really been a pleasure working for you.

Isaac, "the pleasure was all ours. You and Chuma exceeded all expectations. It's been a pleasure," Alice told them. As Isaac and Chuma left their car Jay turns to Alice and explains what they were going to do.

"Babe, this is what we're going to do. My bet is still on Mario and Enzo. As before you shadow Enzo and I'll stick with Mario. We're going to stay in The Beverly Hotel, we still have much of the money that Wainsford gave us. In the bar they had a few pamphlets on New York. Places to eat, site seeing and where to stay. I picked The Beverly because it was only a block from the Waldorf. We should be able to watch their hotel pretty easy. It's a little pricey, almost Thirty dollars."

Inside of the station they said their farewells to the opera company and to Major Hart, then made their way to hail a cab. Jay figured that him and Alice should be at the hotel in no more than fifteen-minutes. The train still have to unload all their luggage on all the gear for the opera.

"Where to Mack," asked the cab driver in his distinctive New York accent. Jay replied, "125 East 50$^{\text{th}}$ street."

"Oh, The Beverly. Sure thing," the driver answered back. They pulled up to the hotel. Jay knew that it was close to the Waldorf, but he didn't know how close. The hotels where catty corner from each other. It only took the about seven-minutes to arrive at the hotel. After checking into the hotel, then went by the Waldorf to scope it out. They wanted to check out how many exits there where. There were a few, but they figured that Mario and Enzo would just leave from the front of the hotel. They made their way back to their hotel. Jay went to the desk to get their key. The desk told him that their luggage was already in their room. When they checked in Jay asked the clerk, "if possible, would we be able to get a corner room facing Lexington and 50$^{\text{th}}$?" They got their corner room on the 8$^{\text{th}}$ floor. Jay wanted to keep an eye on the Waldorf to see when the opera company got to the hotel. The each ordered a beer from room service. Jay put a chair by the window and watch with his binoculars. The groups buses arrived around one-hour later. If everyone in the opera followed S.O.P, "STANDERED OPERATING PERCIDURE", They'll all get to their rooms. Stop for a quick lunch. Then do what they pleased. They had two-days to kill before the performance.

Jay called over to Alice, "Alice they're here. There's a taxi stand right at the front of the hotel. We'll go get something to eat, then make our way downstairs."

"Sounds good, I'm starving." Alice answered back. They waited for about a half-hour then made the way to the restaurant.

After dinner they went downstairs and sat on a bench reading a paper. Forty-minutes later Mario and Enzo both hailed a cab. They got into the cab then got out. That confused Jay for a moment. Mario and Enzo started to walk. They went up Lexington and made a right on 49th street. So, Jay and Alice started to follow keeping around a half-block distance. They crossed Madison with the sleuths right behind. They can see them make a right on to 5th Ave. when Jay got to 5th Avenue, he noticed that Mario and Enzo went into Saks Fifth Avenue. Jay wasn't waiting around for them to finish shopping. So, they made their way back to The Beverly. They both decided that the rest of the day they weren't going to be P.I.'s the rest of the day. Now they were just a couple on vacation in the Big City. They sat at the hotels bar for a while, then went upstairs to their room. They weren't going to be P.I.'s today, but every half hour he would get his binoculars, just to take a look. Tomorrow they were going to get up early, so they can keep an eye on the Waldorf. Then around 10:30 they would take up the surveillance.

They had lunch and dinner in their room. At 1100 they decided to go to bed. There really wasn't any sleeping in the first hour-and-a-half. After they went to bed, Jay started to have one of his nightmares. It was great that Alice would always be by his side, so she could calm him down quickly. Alice always held him tight while sleeping. As she lied there, she was thinking to herself. "Why the hell did I take so long to tell him how I felt. He's the best thing that has happened to me." She finally fell asleep.

The alarm rung at 0630. "Alice rise and shine!" Alice put her pillow over her head and mumbled, "that's easy for you to say, I still need my beauty sleep!"

"Hurry up I'm calling room service to order breakfast. We have a long day ahead of us." Room service didn't open until 0700. So, while waited the went to take a shower. After the shower they got dressed. Jay called room service for breakfast. After breakfast they made their way to the lobby, Jay bought two newspapers and gave one to Alice, then proceeded to go outside to sit on the bench that was in front of their hotel. They started to read the papers. The temperature was about seventeen degrees out, with a cool breeze. Jay didn't count on the amount of people on the street and car traffic. He was hoping that he would be able to see someone leaves the Waldorf. Jay decided to take a break. Alice already had lunch. He decided to take ten-minutes. When he returned, he asked Alice, "anything yet?" it was now 1245. "Nothing yet."

Just as Alice started to go back inside of the hotel, she glances to her left, when she noticed Mario standing in front of the Waldorf, ready to hail a cab. "Jay, don't look now, but it looks like Mario is ready to leave."

"Thanks," said Jay. Jay hailed a cab. "Where to?" Asked the cabby. "Not sure yet. See that cab that's leaving the Waldorf? Follow that cab. Number 713. There's a saw buck for you if you don't lose him. Where do you think he's going?"

"If I didn't know any better, it looks like he's headed to Brooklyn, answered."

The driver was right he was heading to Brooklyn. The cab stayed at least 3 car lengths behind Mario's cab. His cab even went past the Brooklyn Naval Yard. That brought him memories. Mario's cab turned at Halsey Street. The cab stopped in front of a Brownstone. There was an Italian restaurant right across the street from the Brownstone.

"Driver let me off at that restaurant, the LunAtico," Jay said to the driver. Jay got out and entered the restaurant. He got a seat by a window. Jay didn't have a good view, so he finished his drink and left to go outside. There was a big tree right in front of the house that Mario went into. He went to stand by the tree. The only problem the tree had a small trunk, so he was a little exposed. Jay could see movement inside. He was thinking that it may be a meeting of some sort. All of a sudden Mario looks out the window and sees Jay behind the tree. At first, he thought that he was seeing things. No, it was definitely Jay. Mario goes outside to see why he's there. "Jay, what are you doing here?" Mario asked. Jay had to think quick.

"Mario, I thought that was you. I asked a cab driver for a good Italian restaurant, he mentioned the LunAtico. I was nursing a beer before I ordered, then I saw you enter the house, talk about a coincidence. So, Mario who lives here," Jay asked.

Mario didn't skip a beat and said, "my brother lives here. Him my sister-in-law and their 2-year-old son. So, you coming in or what?"

Jay was thinking, this could be good or very bad. Jay said, "sure I'm coming in." While he was walking up the stairs, he had his hand close to his .45. Jay entered the Brownstone. As he walked in, met Mario's brother and his sister- in-law. It just so happened that his siter-in-law's name was Angela. He looked around the room, on the fireplace mantel was a picture. Jay walked over to the photo to get a better look. To Jay's surprise, it was a picture of a Marine Lieutenant. Jay asked, "who's the Marine?"

Angela answered with pride in her voice, "that's my son, Robert. He's stationed in California. He's a lieutenant. He was so proud being Marine."

Jay asked Mario, "Mario, tell me that he's stationed at the Naval Yard in Coronado. That's why you went to the Naval Base to see your nephew. That's a relief. Don't get excited or anything. Me and Alice thought that you were an Italian spy working for Mussolini. Sorry."

"Jay don't worry about that. Mussolini is not a friend of ours. If I, could I'd kill him myself. He's destroying Italy. If I didn't know better, I'd think that he murdered Giovanni. Giovanni was a good man. He would have defected except he has family; he was afraid of what they might do to his family if he defected."

Angela asked Jay, "you have to have dinner with us. If you want an original Italian dinner, you're at the right place." She started to make spaghetti and meat balls. Jay and Mario started talking about Giovanni.

"Giovanni told me how you two met. If you weren't there, he might have been dead," said Mario.

"Did he ever tell you that the very same day, Giovanni saved my live. Shooting at a German officer that was ready to shoot me in back of the head. He didn't kill the German, just stung his had a little. I'm trying to think of the German's name. I just can't think of it. I'm sure that it will come back to me sooner or later. Question, what's Enzo's deal? He was on my list too."

"Well, you know that Enzo is Giovanni's cousin, too? Enzo loved Giovanni, they were competitive to each other, they always respected one another."

"I heard stories that he was a ladies' man. That he slept with both your wives."

"He did, but we're Italians, you might say it's in our blood. That's when he was many years younger. Me and Enzo weren't married at that time. We had a double wedding a few months later. As far as I know he never slept with a married man."

They all sat down to eat. Angela knew how to make him like he was one of the family. After dinner he took Mario aside. "Mario, whatever you do not, do not tell anyone that I was still in New York. As far as anyone knows me and Alice went to Jersey to visit my sister. I will be going to the Carnegie Hall, at you last performance. I have to do some snooping around. I have to find out who killed him. So, MUMS the word."

Mario answered, "I don't know this mum. Jay answered, "Mum means not to say anything, don't even tell anyone associated with the opera. I want to see the looks on their faces when we walk in to the after party."

"Okay Jay, you can depend on me."

After their little talk Jay left and took a cab back to Manhattan. There was a lot of traffic on the way back. It took almost three-hours to get back to the hotel. When he got back to the hotel Alice was sitting outside.

He asked Alice, "Have you been here all day?"

"No, I followed Enzo a few times, one time I thought he saw me. The only thing that he did was go shopping. He must have stopped in every store in New York. He must have spent two-hundred-dollars today. How about you?"

"Well, I followed him to Brooklyn. He went into this house. I watched the house, then I broke the Cardinal rule of being a P.I. He saw me. He waved me over. He invited me in. That made me a little nervous, I had no idea what I was walking into. Well, I did find out one thing. We can take Mario and Enzo off our suspect list. When he went to the Naval Base at Coronado, he went to visit his nephew. He's a Lieutenant in the Corps. A good-looking kid. Tomorrow, we'll go to the Hall when the opera was on stage, and we'll do what you mentioned when we were in Florida. We will search all the luggage on the loading dock. Hopefully, we'll find something if we don't, well, we'll see."

The went to their room. They both got undressed and went to take a shower. After the show they went to bed for about an hour, they weren't sleeping. After doing what all good private eyes do, they got up and dressed then went down to the bar. Jay had a beer, this time Alice had a beer, also.

Jay laid out his plan, "We'll get there at the start of their show. Then we should have plenty of time to search everyone's luggage. I really do hope that we find something. If we do, we'll go up to the reception room and make ourselves known. They opera starts at 1830 (6:30) tomorrow, we will search every piece of luggage that's there, even Mario's and Enzo's."

They left the bar at about 2315. They went back to bed. This time to sleep. It seems like since him and Alice got together, he dreams were gone. He still dreamt of Angela, but they were good dreams. He doesn't dream of her every night, but he still does. They woke at 0730, took another shower, then went down to breakfast. They weren't talking that much. They both were wondering what was going to happen today. If they don't find the killer, then he got away with murder. Failure wasn't in Jay's vocabulary. The rest of the day they just relaxed listening to Guy Lombardo on the radio. At 1700 they went down to dinner. This time they did talk.

"So, Jay what do you think is going to happen tonight?" Jay replied, "I don't really know. I just hope we find something, like papers a map anything. If we don't find out anything by the time the opera is finished, then we're "FINISHED". So, cross your fingers."

"I'd cross my toes if I could. I got faith in you; I have a feeling that we are going to find something."

After dinner they went down to get a cab. The cab driver asked, "where to buddy?"

"Carnegie Hall, there's no rush. When we get there drop us off at the rear, by the loading docks. We're meeting some friends there."

The cab dropped them off at the rear of the building. Jay paid the cab driver, $6.00 and Jay gave him a $5.00 tip. They made their way up the loading docks stairs. All of a sudden Alice got down and started to pick the lock. Jay looked at her with astonishment. He never knew she could pick a lock.

"Where the hell did you learn that? What were you before you came to work with me, a jewel thief?" Jay asked.

Alice answered, "you'll be surprised what I can do. If you're a bad guy, don't mess with me. I can take care of myself."

It took her only eight seconds to pick the lock. They could hear the opera starting. They made their way to where the luggage was being stored before they made the buses. To take the to the USS Manhattan. They stated to inspect the luggage. After an hour they only had two pieces to search. They searched one, found nothing. They didn't find anything in the last piece of luggage. As they started to walk away, disgusted Alice turned around and looked at the last piece of luggage.

"Jay, do you notice anything different at the last trunk we searched?"

Jay turned and looked. Jay said, "I must be losing it. I don't see anything different with that piece."

Alice answered without missing a beat, "and you call yourself a detective! Does that trunk look a little bigger on the outside than it did on the inside"

"Well, I'll be, you're right. Must be five inches difference.

They went back to the trunk and researched it. This time they took everything out of it. Jay knocked on the bottom of the truck, the trunk had a false bottom. Jay took up the false bottom and almost had a heart attack. Inside they found plans of military bases, blueprints of the new B-17, the M1 rifle and plans of the railroads Horseshoe Curve near Altoona, Pennsylvania.

They weren't looking at the names on the luggage. They both almost went into cardiac arrest when they saw the name on the trunk.

Jay said, "okay lets go and watch our last opera. Then we'll go to the after party." Alice agreed.

They made their way to the auditorium, sat all the way in the back. They watched their last opera. After the opera they made their way to the cast going away and after party. They waited awhile before they went upstairs. Jay wanted to make sure that all their props and costumes were packed up. The stagehands were taking down all the props and packed up the costumes. In a half-hour they made their way up to the party. They stayed on the other side of the door for a few minutes Just as they were about to do a toast on the memory of Giovanni.

Jay and Alice entered the room. Everyone had a strange look on their faces, like they just saw a ghost.

The Major raised his glass and said a few words. "This toast is for Giovanni, who isn't with us anymore."

Jay spoke up, "very touching toast. I want to tell you all a little story on how I met Giovanni. Me and my spotter were near the Belleau Wood area. On our way back to meet up with our unit I saw a figure that was ready to execute another soldier. I didn't know if it was a German ready to execute a deserter or a prisoner. Whoever it was I wasn't going to let him be executed. They were around three-hundred-yards away. I took a prone position, took aimed and took the shot hitting the figure in the front of his neck forcing his head backward as he fell backward. I started to make my way to the spot where this happened. It took me almost an hour to get to the area. I finally made it, I noticed that the one I shot was German. I had no idea if the German took a shot. I looked at the man lying on the ground. I didn't recognize the uniform. Wasn't English or American. I didn't see any blood, so I walked over to the soldier and turned him over. At that point I noticed that it was an Italian uniform. The Italian was plying dead and doing a bad job of it. When I told him that the German was dead, he finally opened his eyes. I helped him up, as he got to his feet, he looked over at the body the German was on his back, but his head was looking at both of us. A little weird. I finally caught up with the rest of my unit. They were in pursuit of a small company of Germans. Near this farmhouse we started to receive fire. The Germans took cover behind the wall in front of the farmhouse. Sargent Morris lobbed a grenade behind the wall. We waited a fer minutes before we stated to make our way towards the farmhouse. All of a sudden, we started to get firing from an opened window on the second floor. Two rounds were fired, one round miss, but the other round hit my spotter in his right eye. Killing him instantly. A

Marine shot at the widow. The firing stopped. We made our way to the wall. Sargent Morris peaked around the wall. He noticed that all the Germans were down. We found six German were dead, three were wounded. A Marine went into the farmhouse, he took four steps up the stairs and lobbed a grenade over the banister. After the grenade exploded and the dust and smoke cleared, he went the rest of the way upstairs. The sniper was down, the corporal took two steps into the bedroom. All of a sudden, the German turned and took a shot at the Corporal, missing. The Corporal raise his Springfield rifle and shot him right in the center of his chest, killing him. We all gathered in front of the farmhouse. The Marines were checking out the dead and wounded. Giovanni's back was toward the front door. When Giovanni drew his pistol and took a shot at one of the Germans playing dead. He was about to shoot me in the back. Giovanni shot the pistol out of his hand knocking a chip out of the handgrip. The German playing dead was the company commander. Two Marines secured him. The German would rather die than taken prisoner. He didn't get his wish and spent the war in a prisoner of war camp in England. I could get over how good his English was. He didn't even have an accent. Can't remember if he was a Captain or a Major. One thing I do remember was his name. "CPT or MAJOR Wilhelm Reinhardt, or should I say Major William Hart?"

Har spoke up, "are you out of your mind. I've been in the Army sixteen-years. My family owns a farm suppling the government with meat and milk.

Jay said, "I know your family were farmers, that's why you speak such good English. The only thing that I can figure out is that you must have been in Germany, maybe visiting friends or family when the war broke out. Being a good German, you decided to enlist. I'm not sure how you managed to get a commission." Hart turned and started to walk away. "I searched everyone's baggage and guess what I found."

Meanwhile Dottie was just standing there taking in the situation. Hart turned around nearly hitting Jay on his left side. As Hart ran through the door Jay took a shot shattering the glass in the door. Jay started after him. The cast members just stood there in shock. After Jay made his way out to the hallways Dottie pulled a Luger from her bag.

She said, "nobody move." Alice wasn't that far from Dottie, in a split- second Alice turned and kicked the gun out of her hand. Then gave her a right-cross right to her jaw. She pulled a wire from one of the lamps and tied her up. Then she made her way out to the hallway, looking for Jay and Hart. She sees them going upstairs to the catwalks. Hart turned around taking pot shots at Jay. The rounds were ricochet of the steel framework. Jay was getting closer to Hart. Finally, Jay got close enough to grab Hart's leg Hart kicked Jay in the head with his free leg. Jay was startled, but otherwise not really hurt. They were about seventy feet above the stage. Jay finally grabbed a hold of his belt pulling him down on the catwalk. Hart turned around and kicked Jay in the chest knocking him back against a steel railing. Jay countered with a left hook knocking Hart back. Hart got the upper hand. He was able to get Jay in a headlock. Hart had a tight squeeze on Jay's neck. Jay knew that he had to do something and fast. Jay remembered that a sailor gave Jay a new Zippo, Jay reached in his pocket and grabbed the lighter. Jay started to get weaker. Jay got the Zippo out lit it and put the lighter up to Hart's arm that was around Jay's neck. Jay stated to smell the fabric on Hat's uniform, when the flame burnt away on Hart's sleeve, he gave out a loud scream or grunt. Hart released the head lock and fell back to the opposite steel railing, at that time gave him a shot to the stomach, when he bent over Jay gave him a right uppercut knocking him back and over the railing. Hart grabbed a hold of the railing.

He yelled out this, "I should have killed you in the baggage car."

"You should have, but you didn't," Jay replied. Then Jay walked over to Hart and stepped on his hand causing Hart to lose his grip. He fell seventy feet to the stage below. Jay was glad that he didn't fall on one of the stagehands. Jay walked back to the party room. When he entered the room, he noticed that Alice had everything under control. Jay apologized to the Opera Company, for thinking that someone in the Opera was the cause of Giovanni's murder. Alice put Dottie in a chair and waited for the police and the FBI show up. Alice called the police, told them what happened, in turn the police called the FBI.

Jay also told them about what happened in France in 1918, and he thought that Giovanni recognized him. When Hart or Reinhardt finally figured that Giovanni has recognized him, Hart had no other choice but to kill Giovanni.

Jay also said, "I didn't recognize Hart until we searched his luggage and found all the blueprints and maps that he had."

Jay explained to the authorities exactly what happened and why. He started from the beginning all the way to what happened tonight. The FBI Agent said, "Mr. Jax you did your county a great service. Thank you.

Jay replied, "once a Marine Always A Marine. I only did what I had to." Alice said all's well that ends well."

Jay and Alice finally made it to Woodbridge.

# Epilog

When Jay and Alice left to go back to San Francisco he decided to take his sister back with him. Being that Alice and him were now partners they needed a secretary. Three weeks after they returned to San Francisco they were married. Mr. Wainsford hosted the wedding, making it one of the biggest events since his wedding. Jay and Alice went back to being Private Eyes. Jax and Jax became one of the biggest Private Investigation companies in San Francisco.

### *Until Next Time*